Peter Lucy is a writer and historian living in Somerset, UK. He has had a lifelong interest in historic arms and armour and enjoys live action roleplay and costumed historic interpretation. He has a master's degree in history from De Montfort University and a PhD from Cranfield University. He has served on operations as an army reservist and has worked extensively in the film industry.

For Mylah and Arlo

Peter Lucy

GUARDIANS

AUSTIN MACAULEY PUBLISHERS™

LONDON • CAMBRIDGE • NEW YORK • SHARJAH

A CIP catalogue record for this title is available from the British Library.

ISBN 9781398470163 (Paperback)
ISBN 9781398470170 (ePub e-book)

www.austinmacauley.com

First Published 2023
Austin Macauley Publishers Ltd®
1 Canada Square
Canary Wharf
London
E14 5AA

With thanks to Matt Pennington for his kindness and support; to Angela Clarke, Joan Rotherham, Nikki Richardson, and Felix Vogel for being the reading team; to Theadora Dane for the cover illustration; to Luke Evans and the Austin Macauley Publishers team for making this book happen; and especially to the players, game makers, crew, and organisers for being an inspiration.

Table of Contents

Author's Note

'The only thing I would want of any artist who is inspired by Empire in any way is that they do the best by their art that they can.'

Matt P., July 2021

I

An angry wind was pushing at the wet fabric of the tents and tugging at the banner which thrashed and snapped, pulling madly against its staff.

'I don't understand,' said Thaddeus.

'It's quite simple. The company is yours now.' The older man looked drawn, careworn. Without his uniform, his armour, in the simple robe of a pilgrim, he seemed vulnerable. Thaddeus had never seen him like this. It was sad.

'But why?'

'It's time for me to go.' Lazarus stared into the distance his eyes unfocussed. The wind was blowing ragged curtains of rain between the rows of tents. He shook his head sadly.

'Are you wounded?'

'In a sense, I suppose. Perhaps you could say that I have lost something.'

'What? What have you lost?'

'The thing I believed in.'

'But we need you. The company needs you – I need you.'

'You don't, and what the company needs is fresh leadership.' Lazarus smiled and slapped Thaddeus's shoulder: 'The energy of youth. And faith too – make the most of belief while you still have it my young friend.' He sighed and shook his head. 'I've given away all my clothes and my armour. Forgive me, I was foolish, you should have had the helmet with the Magpie's wings.'

'No! That was always you.'

'You're probably right. You need to make your own way, create your own impression.'

'Why me though?'

'You're the best of us, that's why I picked you as my second-in-command. Your father would have been proud of you.'

'He wasn't much of a soldier.'

'He placed value on a life. He did everything he could to keep us all alive. Too much perhaps, but his heart was good.'

'The company has a strong reputation now.'

'Yes, build on it.' Lazarus placed his hand on Thaddeus's forehead. 'May the Paragons preserve you Thaddeus, and your company. Walk in Virtue my friend.'

'And you.' Thaddeus stepped back and saluted, his head bowed, clenched fist to his chest.

The older man put up his hood, picked up his staff, and stepped out into the wind and rain.

'Lazarus!' Thaddeus called. 'Will we see you again?'

'No,' said Lazarus, 'I am retired!' He walked slowly through the double line of tents. There were two sentries, alert, watchful, the wind tugging at their cloaks, their hoods up against the rain, armed with shield and spear. They bowed their heads to their former commander; he gripped the shoulder of each, exchanged a few words and shared a smile with them, and walked out of the camp.

Thaddeus sat down on the folding camp stool. Lazarus had left a small, neat pile of papers, held against the wind by a heavy pewter medal commemorating the raid on Dubhtraig. Thaddeus looked through them: pay returns, allowances and deductions, list of effectives and sick and wounded, weekly orders. The company was his, he had his own command.

It was a sunny Friday morning, summer on the cusp of autumn, deep in the English countryside. A queue of assorted vehicles stood nose to tail quietly idling, tucked into the side of a farm track, and stretching back half a mile to the main road. They were being processed through a big grey steel farm gate, ticked off, one at a time. Many were small, well-used hatchbacks, packed to the roof with kit, there were some hired minibuses, some camper vans, and various cargo vans. There were too, smart four-by-fours driven by worried but supportive parents, delivering enthusiastic student-age beginners to their first event. Dust hung in the air, thickening every time a big farm vehicle was waved past pulling a trailer, or carrying something huge and heavy on front forks. Gwin eased her laden hatchback forward one car-length. Beside her Beth was engrossed on her phone. She looked up. 'The field's looking good, really dry.' She showed Gwin her phone; there was a picture of some grass. Gwin nodded, paused, dropped the handbrake, and moved forward another car-length.

Minibuses were unloading, turning around, and going back to pick up more players determined enough to travel in by train. A long stream of pedestrians was overtaking the line of vehicles, being checked in, and then struggling onward, burdened with backpacks, carrier bags, and fighting swords, shields and battle-axes thinly disguised inside black plastic bin bags. There were no police, no crowd barriers, no security heavies, just three thousand people with a common interest, determined to have a great weekend, thrilled to meet up with their friends. Gwin, who worked in film production, and therefore knew a thing or two about setting up on location, was astounded at the way the whole thing seemed to run on an endless reserve of patience and good humour. She was impressed, and they hadn't even got through the gate.

They were still three cars back when a young man with a red baseball cap and a clipboard came up to Gwin's window and checked them off against his list. There was the usual kerfuffle over Gwin's surname. 'Not Weaver, Weyve-Ross, it's hyphenated.' But there she was, and so was Beth, paid-up, ready to play. She was handed a piece of paper to put in her windscreen, with her player number on it.

'Have you been before?' asked the redcap.

'No,' said Gwin.

'Yes,' said Beth, without looking up from her phone. 'I have.'

'There's a one-way system, put your hazards on, keep your speed down, and follow the cars right, up past the woods, then left along the main drag. Highguard is up on the right, look for the Sentinel Gate. Drop your stuff off, then follow the one-way out through the out-of-character area, and park up in that field over there.' He pointed to a field to their front, which was already filling with rows of parked vehicles and tents of every size, shape, and colour.

'Thank you,' said Gwin, totally confused.

'Don't worry,' said Beth, 'I know exactly where we're going.'

They turned right at a huge log, with a couple more crew sitting on it, then bumped forward along a track and through another gate. 'Welcome to Anvil, the meeting place of the

Empire,' said Beth. The track was laid with wood chippings, but the small wheels of Gwin's little hatchback were finding every pothole and bump and the car was pitching and rolling as if they were at sea. 'Imperial Orcs and Navarr,' said Beth, pointing to the woods they were passing; they climbed, then dipped down, past some rather cute plywood buildings, like cottages. 'In-character loos,' said Beth. 'Go left here.'

As they took the road through the heart of the site, Gwin's resolve started to drain away. It wasn't that she hadn't known what she was letting herself in for. Beth was a committed larper, live action role play gamer, and talked of little else. Gwin had listened patiently to the endless talk, looked at the photos, gone online, become curious, been persuaded, joined up, created an account, and created a character, but nothing had prepared her for the scale of the actual event. They were at the heart of it now, and hundreds of in-character tents, mostly buff-coloured bell tents, but interspersed with striped medieval tentage, canopies, awnings and marquees, and a few wooden structures, stretched out in all directions. There were shops, cafes, meeting places, it was totally overwhelming. Gwin wondered if she could drop Beth off and escape, she could tell her she would be back to collect her on Sunday afternoon…

'Dawn,' said Beth, still pointing out the ten national contingents that made up the Empire. 'There are the Marchers, with the Varushkans behind. That's the League.' They turned off the road at the area reserved for the nation of Highguard, and Gwin carefully drove over the grass through a forest of standing tents and ones in the process of being put up. They found a quietly spoken player called Mark, who had a map. 'You two are two three-metre bell tents, in the new chapter?' asked Mark. They nodded. 'Okay, your spots are here and here.' He pointed to a clear patch of grass.

The gang were all there already and overjoyed to see Beth. There were hugs, Gwin stood by, self-consciously, and was introduced. She forgot everyone's name immediately, except Russell, an unmissably huge figure with wild black hair and an unkempt beard, leaning heavily on a stick. The chapter had its own big tent, and a table and benches, and a steel fire pit, and cold boxes with drinks and snacks. The smaller bell tents clustered around the big chapter tents – there were a dozen or so chapters of various sizes making up the national contingent for Highguard – there were flags and banners, and black and white bunting, the Highborn being rather conservative compared to the other nations.

Gwin and Beth started pulling their kit out of the car, the two big bags with the tents in them were right at the bottom, under all the lighter stuff and the fragile bits and the food. 'Do many of these people work in film or TV?' asked Gwin.

'A few, not many though,' said Beth.

Gwin shook her head. 'We should sack our locations people and hire this lot instead. It's incredible.'

'I always think it goes to show what can happen when you just treat people like grown-ups and let them get on with it' – Beth grinned – 'which is a bit ironic when we're all here to spend three days playing make-believe.'

They left their kit in a pile and jumped back in the car. 'Will our stuff be okay?' asked Gwin. Beth nodded. 'Fine, the others will keep an eye on it.'

They got back on the track and headed right towards another gate. 'Urizen,' said Beth, indicating players from the next nation along, who were busy erecting a big Japanese-style arch in the middle of their camp. 'And there's the Brass Coast.'

Through the gate they stopped by a huge skip. To their front was a row of mobile catering stands, doing everything from noodles to bratwurst. 'This is out-of-character, once you're through that gate you can relax, you're outside the game. Out-of-character food stalls, the first aid centre, and that's GOD.' She pointed to a huge marquee on their right.

'God?'

'Games Operation Desk. That's where the game is run from, we'll go there and pick up our player packs. There's computers in there too, so if your character gets killed you can log on to your account and create a new one.'

'Which way?'

'Go left…Toilets and showers,' said Beth as they drove past.

They parked in the field they had been shown when they arrived, which was nearly full of vehicles and tents. 'Out-of-character camping,' said Beth, 'we're outside of the game here, obviously.'

Their tents were up and Beth and Gwin were in the GOD marquee, queuing for their player packs. 'Nine-seven-one-oh-point-one,' said Gwin, reading the number she had written on the back of her hand.

'Guardian Thaddeus?'

'That's right.'

She was handed a fat white envelope with her name and number on it. 'I can't believe they do one of these for every player,' said Gwin, as they sat on a step by the big skip and tore open their envelopes. Inside was a sheet of paper with all the details of Guardian Thaddeus, Gwin's character, some little plastic ingots and a few small coins. 'What are these?'

Beth looked at the ingots. 'Green iron. Okay, so to be at Anvil, which is here, for the solstice, which is now, you have to be one of the great and the good of the Empire. Well, not necessarily good, and only great enough to have an independent income – but movers and shakers though. Your character's resource is a military unit, and that unit has earned him some income. Because you're a new player they've picked something random, green iron, and given you a little money to get started.'

Gwin examined the ingots. 'What do I do with these?'

'Anything you like – trade them or sell them to get into the trading game, donate them to a good cause, give them to the chapter benefactor – that's the person who trades for the chapter – so they can make them part of a bigger deal. Basically, it gets you engaged and playing.'

'And the money?'

Beth looked. 'Seven one ring pieces and one five ring piece – twelve rings. Okay, well there are twenty rings to a crown, and eight crowns to a throne. A crown can probably get you a meal, so you haven't got enough to retire on yet, but it's a start. You need money if you want to get something, like getting a mage to cast a ritual to strengthen your armour. You can save up over events, sell stuff like your green iron, do things for people, or borrow. Basically, more interactions, more play. You can buy real-life stuff with your coins too – people sell bracelets and muffins and all sorts.'

Gwin shook her head, it was like she just stepped into another world.

A little later Beth dropped Gwin off at the new player briefing. Gwin was expecting mostly student-age newbies, and there were plenty of those, but also young families, in fact people from every age group. There were a couple of new players who obviously imagined the whole thing was a cosplay event for Dungeons and Dragons and had turned out in elaborate and fragile-looking costumes with lots of exposed flesh, which would look awesome in some convention centre, but were going to get pretty bedraggled over three days of getting in and out of tents and being lived-in full-time. Gwin was starting to appreciate that the event was much more like historical re-enactment, in that you were part of a group to take part, and you had to be able to live and operate in your kit. Luckily, she had quite a lot of experience in that regard.

The briefing was followed later by a practical session on fighting, for those who wanted to take part in the battles and skirmishes. By the end of it all, Gwin realised they had been given just about enough information to keep their heads above water; the game was mind-bogglingly rich, complex, and detailed. Part of her wanted to run back to the tent and curl up at the bottom of her sleeping bag, and part of her wanted to pull on her costume and chainmail and crowd-surf. She didn't know whether to be thrilled or terrified.

Gwin decided not to head straight back to the chapter, and instead went to explore the traders' stalls – tented shops crammed with weapons, armour, leatherwork, clothes, anything and everything a larper might need. There was a narrow passage between a sword-seller and a huge shop called 'the Emporium' and at the end was a single tent, a "Burgundian", a tall narrow cylinder of striped cloth, with a pointed roof, like something from a medieval manuscript. She could hear the sound of a hammer against metal, she peered through the doorway, there was a section of tree trunk in the middle of the tent, with a vaguely T-shaped piece of iron stuck in the top of it. On this an armourer was resting a steel collar, a gorget, tapping at it with a slim hammer. Afternoon sunlight through the tent's doorway shone on the bright steel, the man was in shadow.

'*Busy hammers closing rivets up*?' Gwin quoted.

He looked up and smiled. 'Indeed!'

'You have a very small anvil.'

'It's called a stake, and no one has ever complained.'

'I wondered if you would be here.'

'Couldn't stay away. I have something for you.' He put down the gorget and rummaged in the dark depths of the tent. There were two bundles, wrought steel wrapped in cloth. He handed them over to Gwin. There was a pair of greaves, armour for the legs, not the cheap kind like football shin guards, but shaped to encase the leg from knee to ankle, fitted with hinges and catches, real armour. They even had articulated defences for the knees. And there were vambraces, arm defences, again shaped, fitted to the whole lower arm, with pieces to protect the elbow.

'They are beautiful,' said Gwin.

'Try them.'

'Will they fit me?'

'They should. There are some boots too – shoes really.'

The armour did fit, like a second skin. He helped her by doing up the swivelling catches that fastened the pieces around her legs and arms, and the leather straps at the knees and elbows.

Gwin flexed her arms, then stood, walked, and stretched to test the greaves. 'I love them, but it'll take me a year's salary to pay for them. Something to save up for.'

He shook his head. 'No, it's a gift; you're going to need them.'

'I couldn't.'

'They only fit you.'

She carefully took off the armour and examined it, working the knee and elbow pieces, watching how the slim lames of steel slid over one and other. 'I love the poleyns and couters,' she said.

The armourer was delighted, he leant back and closed his eyes with a look of bliss. 'I could have made you in a computer!'

'You did.'

'True.'

'Okay. Thank you – really, thank you. Am I supposed to take these now?' She was holding the greaves and vambraces in her arms, an awkward mass of shaped steel and dangling leather straps, and her new medieval shoes in one hand.

'You had better, I can't promise I'll be here later.'

'Okay. Well. Thank you, they are gorgeous.'

He smiled. 'Enjoy the event.'

When Gwin got back to her tent, the armour was a sensation. 'Somebody has blown their holiday money!' said Beth.

'It's a gift, from a friend. He made them for me.'

'I didn't know you knew anyone else here,' said Beth, slightly miffed.

'He sort of pops up, I guess he knew I was coming.'

Everyone crowded around and demanded she try the armour on.

'How long till time-in?' Gwin asked.

'An hour,' said Russell. 'There'll be a skirmish, if you want to try your armour…'

'Just, for goodness' sake don't get killed!' said Beth. 'There's nothing more dreadful than losing your first character on the first skirmish of your first event.'

'Does happen though,' said Russell.

'Okay, I'll do it – and I'll be careful, I'll keep my head down and stay at the back. I just hope I can remember all the stuff from this afternoon about fighting. It seemed quite complicated.'

'Don't forget you've got to do hair and makeup too,' said Beth. 'Do you need a hand with the binder?'

'I'm trying tape that's made for the job, it's much lower maintenance and seems to be a lot more comfortable. I've worn a binder a lot and it nearly kills me, with the tape I could even go all Orlando Bloom and have my shirt open to the waist. Not that that's really my character's look, fun to have the option though.'

Sometime later Gwin emerged from her tent, dressed mostly in character, and dragged out her armour and see-through ScreenFace professional makeup bag. She was already wearing the second-hand hauberk – a long chainmail shirt with elbow-length sleeves – that she had bought on eBay. It was incredibly heavy, and worn over another purchase, a padded gambeson jacket, together they were hot, heavy, and constricting.

'Put your belt on,' said Beth, 'and hitch the hauberk up inside it a bit, that way you take some of the weight on your hips, and it's not all hanging on your shoulders.'

Gwin put her makeup bag on the trestle table and set up her mirror, then wrestled with the chainmail and her long sword belt, which had to be buckled, then fed back through and over the belt so that the loose end hung straight down from her waist. Sorted, she tried to focus and remember the master class she'd had from the makeup team at work – who had absolutely relished turning her into an anime boy. Previously she had made do with short hair, a binder, a tan from outdoor living, and the peak of her cap pulled down low – but that had been another time, another place, and a place where nobody was expecting a woman, which helped a lot. She flipped her hair back, and started to add darker skin tone, brow, sharper cheek bones and jaw line. There was a shield propped up against the table. 'Whose is that?' asked Gwin, as she blurred in some powder.

'It's for you,' said Beth, 'the chapter has a pile of spare kit people can borrow. Might stop you getting killed.'

'Thank you!'

Gwin finished hair and makeup and started to buckle on her greaves and vambraces. She fumbled and Beth and Russell had to help her.

'I thought we were supposed to have squires.'

'In your dreams,' said Beth, 'everyone joins the game as a hero, I can only think of one person who ever joined as a squire and worked their way up.'

'Really, who?'

'The Exarch.'

'Wow, from helping people dress to running your own chapter?'

'Yup, and only a few years' playing too.'

Gwin took a few paces to get the feel. 'I can hardly move. Whose idea was this anyway?' She gave a self-conscious smile.

'What's your character's name?' asked Russell, who was now two-thirds dressed as a mage, a cambion with tightly twisted black ram's horns which really did look as if they were sprouting out of his thick dark hair.

'Er…Guardian Thaddeus. Your horns look amazing, by the way.'

'Greetings Thaddeus.'

'Er…Greetings,' said Gwin, feeling exactly like Gwin-in-fancy-dress, and not at all like Guardian Thaddeus.

The meeting point for the skirmish was near the great grey arch of the Sentinel Gate, a short walk from Gwin's tent. As she walked, she felt her pace slowing, becoming more uncertain by the minute. She felt ridiculous. People were looking at her. A photographer aimed his camera at her and snapped some shots of her among the tents. She had the wit to ignore the camera and stride purposefully, although she felt anything but. Briefly she was irritated, and then she remembered that photographers were strictly limited at the event and were careful only to take images that captured the best of the action. She felt some confidence returning, and that put a spring in her step. It dawned on her that in her mail and chapter surcoat and polished armour, with her shield and sword, and anime boy hair and makeup, she wasn't Gwin Weyve-Ross in her North Face jacket, jeggings and Converses anymore, but Guardian Thaddeus, a formidable and respected Highborn warrior. She struggled to remember Shakespeare's word for a fully dressed man-at-arms. *Accomplished.* Yes, she was accomplished. She squared her shoulders and tried to suppress the butterflies in her stomach.

There was a small group forming by the Sentinel Gate. The huge arch of Anvil's ancient magical portal was a great chunk of set dressing, beautifully made, painted and textured to represent stone, and elaborately carved with arcane symbols. It loomed over the sea of tents, which were on ground that fell gently away below it. The skirmish was being organised by a boisterous and enthusiastic Dawnish battle captain, looking suitably Pre-Raphaelite-Arthurian in bright silks and polished armour. His skirmishers were a couple more Dawnish, and a Leaguer dressed as a Landsknecht, with parti-coloured hose, a slashed doublet, and a huge two-handed sword. There were three Marchers, probably Wars of the Roses re-enactors to judge by their excellent costumes – simple peasant foot soldiers for sure, but you could tell even the thread stitching their aketon jackets was handmade. The balance was a gaggle of Anglo-Saxon-styled Steinr and fur-and-leather clad Suaq, all from the nation of Wintermark, and probably brand-new players, judging by their basic costume and weapons, and level of nervous excitement.

Gwin hoped to sidle up to the skirmish party and take up a spot at the rear, but the Dawnish battle captain saw her and bounded over. 'Hello!' he said with a big grin. 'I was hoping we'd have some Highborn, we're going to need some heavy armour and shields. Do you know if there are any more of you?'

'No,' said Gwin, 'I mean, no I don't know.' Oh, this was so *awkward.* Everyone else seemed to have slipped easily into their characters, but Gwin was really struggling. Every word Gwin-as-Thaddeus uttered felt forced and uncomfortable.

'I can't remember if we've met,' said the battle captain, and reeled off a long Dawnish name, involving House-something-or-other, that went in one of Gwin's ears and straight out the other.

'Er Guardian Thaddeus, *Brother* Thaddeus,' she said, helping him out.

'Greetings Brother!' said the battle captain and gave Gwin a cheery slap between the shoulder blades that rattled her teeth. 'I need all the shields up at the front. I'm relying on the battle-hardened fighters, half of this mob are just recruits, willing, but completely inexperienced.'

He walked as he talked, steering Gwin to the front of the skirmish party, now forming into a rough column.

'Ah,' said Gwin, then, 'wait, but I'm…' But he was gone. *Oh dear*, thought Gwin.

'Right, listen up!' shouted the battle captain, standing to the flank. The motley column of Imperial heroes shuffled left to face him. 'Raiding parties of Druj…orcs,' he added, for the benefit of new players, 'have been attacking villages and carrying off Imperial citizens to enslave them. The prognosticators have determined that there is a conjunction of the Sentinel Gate that can put us close to one of these raiding parties. Our task is to track and kill the raiders and free the prisoners, bringing them safely back through the gate. The only problem is that the gate is only open for a short time, so we will need to be quick and efficient. Are there any questions?'

Gwin was still pondering 'prognosticators' and only vaguely heard the rest. She swallowed; her mouth was dry. She was beginning to think she might need to go for a pee.

The two Marchers nearest Gwin were looking at her and she looked back, then realised that everyone had drawn their swords, except her. She hauled out Thaddeus's shortsword, hoping no one would see her blushing under her anime boy makeup.

The armour and chainmail were real, but for safety, shields and weapons were built from dense foam, covered with coloured latex, and spray-painted to give a realistic finish. The blades of swords and pole arms were thicker than real ones, partly because they were foam and partly because they contained fibreglass core to keep them rigid, encased in Kevlar fabric to prevent it breaking through the foam and latex and stabbing someone. Gwin was pretty familiar with film props, but even she had to admit the shields and weapons were superb, and surprisingly convincing. Certainly, a million miles away from the giant foam 'boffers' inflicted on American larpers by their health and safety rules. And health and safety *was* definitely a thing – there would be some seven hundred people fighting in the free-play battles on Saturday and Sunday, so there were rules – blows had to be "pulled", no stabbing, no hitting to the face or head, and there were calls too – to indicate particularly savage strikes, like "cleave" or "impale", and the use of magic. Everyone had a number of hit points, and when they had been hit enough times, they bled out, unless a healer got to them in time. Armour like Gwin's increased her hit points.

Which was good.

Probably.

Gwin's head was spinning.

'Go!'

'What?' said Gwin, turning around.

'*GO!*' shouted the wild-eyed Dawnish knight behind her, as she shouldered Gwin out of the way. Gwin was swept through the Sentinel Gate by the column of skirmishers.

II

As she passed through the arch of the gate, Gwin felt something – like walking through the downdraft heaters in the doorway of a big department store in the winter, or, more complicatedly, like jumping into a swimming pool but without getting wet. She had crossed some sort of threshold, and things were a bit strange. The quality of the light was different, the foliage seemed a darker green than she remembered, and it was thicker. The ground was broken and seemed to rise up to the left and right in a way she didn't remember noticing when she was waiting on the other side of the gate.

But the topography and flora were the least of Gwin's worries. Something had happened to her: her body felt unfamiliar, and she seemed to be sharing her mind with someone else. Gwin was panicking, but the other person was completely focussed, controlling their shared body, eyes scanning the undergrowth, left hand loosely gripping their shield, right hand lightly holding their sword, index finger over the cross guard, a grip such as one might use to hold a small bird, the grip of someone who had carried a sword since his tenth birthday, and really, *really* knew how to use one. As the other's consciousness seeped over to Gwin, she realised this was Thaddeus. Not Gwin-as-Thaddeus, tyro role player, but Thaddeus-as-Thaddeus. Gwin had a much higher tolerance for weirdness than most people, but this was pushing even her needle into the red.

Thaddeus looked over to the battle captain. Like everything else, the Dawnish looked similar but different. What struck Gwin was that his sword was a gleaming sliver of wicked steel. She wondered why she hadn't noticed it before, and if she ought to say something. There was no way that would have passed the weapons safety check – he could have someone's eye out. Then Gwin saw that Thaddeus's sword too was a razor-sharp steel version of what they had lined up with at the Sentinel Gate. Slowly she began to grasp that, in some bizarre way, things had become extremely real.

Thaddeus walked on, cautious, alert. Was this what it felt like to be a man? Gwin could sense the weight of heavier bones and extra muscle, a broad, flat chest and shoulders that were so far apart they seemed to be in different postcodes; there was also a subtly different walk and feet that felt huge. She tried to concentrate on walking, and their shared body stumbled awkwardly. 'Take your hands off the wheel,' she told herself, she was just a passenger, she needed to leave this to Thaddeus. Gwin supposed it must be like this travelling in one of those self-driving cars – constantly fighting the urge to grab the controls.

She could feel Thaddeus's thoughts, and knew he wasn't happy. Something was wrong, and the hair on the back of her new thicker male neck prickled as it stood on end.

They moved deeper into the woods, treading warily, like hunters, tracking, cautiously scanning the ground for spoor and sign, scanning the undergrowth for lurking Druj. There wasn't a sound, no birdsong, no startled animals darting out of the way, just a heavy expectant silence.

The battle captain held up a hand for the party to stop, and signalled to close-in. 'We need to push on faster,' he said.

'Death or glory,' said the Dawnish knight with a wry grin.

'Let's hope we're given the choice,' said Thaddeus, drily.

The Dawnish knight gave a quiet laugh. 'I thought you Highborn couldn't wait to rush to the Labyrinth and come back reborn.'

'Yes, and you Dawnish will go charging off after glory and immortal fame and get killed in the process. Personally, I'm always in favour of helping the opposition die for their cause, while I stay alive for mine.'

'This feels all wrong,' said the other Dawnish.

No one said anything. There was nothing to be said – they were all thinking the same thing.

One of the Marchers was squatting down, examining the grass. 'There's no trampling.'

'Odd,' said the Dawnish, 'If they're moving fast and dragging a load of prisoners.'

'Perhaps they didn't come this way?' said the knight. 'Perhaps they're not here?'

'Oh, they're here alright,' said Thaddeus.

The experienced fighters were close enough together to hear each other speak, but were looking outwards, not taking their eyes off the thick greenery. The recruits were in a huddle, eyes on the veterans, hands nervously gripping their weapons, waiting to be told what to do.

'Alright, that's enough,' said the battle captain. 'We have a task; we'll push forward and see if we can catch up with the orcs and the captives. Let's keep moving, but up the pace.'

The skirmish party moved deeper in, pushing on more quickly, following the narrow grassy path through the woods. The experienced fighters at the front held their shields and swords forward, rotating their bodies as their eyes swept the dense undergrowth that lined their path. The recruits looked around, wide eyed, looking but not seeing, and looking at each other for reassurance; a couple of them had already become weary, and rested their weapons on their shoulders. The silence was oppressive, the skirmisher's feet scuffed through the long grass, their armour clattered, baggy clothing swished, and water sloshed in quarter-empty water-skins and bottles – noises that would have gone unnoticed the other side of the Sentinel Gate but sounded loud, intrusive, and unnatural in the silent, shadowed wood.

Gwin saw what Thaddeus saw – the merest flicker of a movement in the corner of his right eye. She would have disregarded it as some forest animal or turned to take a second look. Thaddeus didn't. 'AMBUSH RIGHT!' he bellowed, turned to the right and threw himself forwards. Suddenly ragged, terrifying, painted Druj orcs burst out of the undergrowth almost under their feet. The Druj ambush was compromised – they were waiting for the heavily armed and experienced Imperials in the vanguard to pass, to emerge behind them, outflanking them and falling on the recruits, hitting them on their unshielded side. Now, the experienced fighters, Imperial and Druj, knew the only recourse was to close with the enemy as quickly and violently as possible.

If Gwin's consciousness had been able to grip, it would have been holding on with both hands, because what followed was a white-knuckle ride. It was fascinating, if terrifying, to be able to observe from within, as Thaddeus unleashed twelve years of close-combat training and practical battlefield experience. The first thing Gwin noticed was that everything was widescreen. Thaddeus barely looked at his opponents, and certainly not at their evil-looking weapons. He kept his field of view wide, relying on his peripheral vision. The second thing was that it all happened very, very fast. There was no time to plan and execute, just reflex, training, and instant, deadly action, and everything – sword, shield, knees, elbows – was a weapon.

An orc leapt up and ran at Thaddeus with a large-bladed axe, held double-handed above his head. If he had struck the Highborn, he would have split him from crown to crotch, but as the axe arced down, Thaddeus caught the haft with a sloping parry, his sword deflecting the axe so that it caught on the steel-bound upper edge of his shield, and as it did he slashed across the orc's throat, cutting him to the spine, and he slumped to his knees and toppled sideways, bubbling and spurting blood. Still charging forward Thaddeus shook off the axe. A second orc had a spear, but Thaddeus was moving too fast, already inside its reach, parrying it to one side with the edge of his shield he struck the orc full force with the flat of the shield, knocking her on her back. As Thaddeus ran over her, he drove the point of the shield into the Druj's ribs with a sound that reminded Gwin of standing on a garden snail: a terminal, wet, bursting crunch.

Another orc was standing up, emerging from his hiding place in tall bracken a little further back. He was young, uncertain, on the edge of panic. When he saw the other two felled by the charging Highborn, he hesitated between fight and flight, and that was enough to give Thaddeus the opportunity to throw himself at him. Thaddeus raised his shield under the orc's spear and hit him sliding feet-first, knocking the orc's legs out from under him as his spear glanced harmlessly upwards. Thaddeus was on his back, punching upwards with the cross guard of his sword as the orc fell on top of him. The blow tore open the orc's cheek, and as he let go of his spear and clutched at his face Thaddeus brought the weighted pommel of his sword down on the top of the orc's skull. The blow would have crushed a human skull like an egg, but only stunned the orc. Thaddeus struck him again with an armoured elbow. As the orc rolled over Thaddeus rolled too, up on to his knees and two-handed, drove the point of his sword through the young orc's throat.

Three more Druj turned and fled, vanishing into the bushes. Thaddeus pulled his bloodied sword out the orc and looked around. The two Dawnish had reacted as he had, charging with him straight at the ambushers. The knight was wiping the blade of her sword, having just given a *coup-de-grace* to Thaddeus's second opponent. The other Dawnish was standing over a fourth orc corpse, poised, sword and shield at the ready, scanning the undergrowth ahead of them. Thaddeus noticed that one of the Marchers was down, the others protecting him with their shields. The Leaguer was brandishing his huge sword. In front of him lay an orc, or strictly speaking, two halves of an orc. It was the sort of mighty blow that would be spun into legend by the Dawnish troubadours, but on the day, on the battlefield, what was most noticeable was the steamy pile of grey-green viscera spilling out of the halves, and the smell, neither of which was remotely glamorous.

The Leaguer ducked as an arrow snicked past him, and then a second. The Druj had melted back into the woods and were quite content to stand off and kill them from a distance with venom-tipped arrows or bolts. They had no illusions about heroic one-on-one combat, and would thin the skirmishers out from a distance, then fall on them when they were outnumbered and disadvantaged. The lucky Imperials would die in the fight, the unlucky ones would be kept alive under torture for as long as Druj ingenuity could manage.

The recruits were in a tight knot around a Suaq who was wounded, unsteady on her feet and holding her arm, blood flowing freely through her fingers from a deep gash, and running down beneath her sleeve to drip from her hand, making dark red splatters on the green grass. She was pale and being supported by another Wintermarker. The recruits were not so much terrified as completely confused, trying to process what just happened and work out what they were supposed to be doing. With the best will in the world, they were useless.

The battle captain was with the Marchers, kneeling beside the injured man, who was writing in agony, venom spreading through his veins from an arrow in his thigh. Thaddeus wiped his blade on the orc's robes and walked back to the battle captain. 'We need to fall back immediately,' he said.

'We haven't saved the prisoners.'

'We haven't seen a sign of any prisoners. If they are alive, they could be anywhere in this forest. If we go on, we will all die, and not at all gloriously. This is a trap. It always was a trap.'

The battle captain met the eyes of the Dawnish knight, standing behind Thaddeus, and she nodded. He turned. 'Shields at the rear, we withdraw. I want the wounded through the gate first.'

Gwin was on all fours on the grass, just beyond the Sentinel Gate. She was head down, waiting for Thaddeus to stand, but he was gone, and she realised she was back in control. She struggled to coordinate, dizzy with the experience, disorientated, and shocked by the sudden violence of the battle she had just witnessed. Her body felt different again, slight, gracile. She could probably dance all night – if she could only stand up.

A hand under her arm helped her to her feet. It was the battle captain, the two other Dawnish were with him, smiling at her. 'You sir are a force of nature. We Dawnish salute you!'

Gwin waited for some pithy response from Thaddeus, and then remembered he wasn't there. 'Yes...er...Thank you.' She winced with embarrassment. 'Is everybody alright?'

'We lost one of the Marchers. Venomed arrow, he bled out too fast. The Wintermarker's in the hospital.'

'Er, out-of-character – did anybody get hurt – the orcs?'

The Dawnish player was surprised. 'No, no complaints, although it was a hell of a skirmish to start the weekend. Thought I spotted a few Hema moves there.'

Gwin looked at him blankly.

'You know HEMA – Historical European Martial Arts? That's what you were doing weren't you?'

'What? Oh, ah, yes. Absolutely.'

'In-character – you must come over to the Dawn encampment Brother Thaddeus.'

'Ah, yes, that would be lovely, er, very nice, er, thanks. That is, thank you.'

'I'm going to be leading another skirmish in an hour, will you be joining us?'

'Ah no, thank you – I've got some important business back at the chapter. Perhaps later?'

'I hope so!'

Gwin-as-Thaddeus trudged back to the tents trailing her shield. She felt drained and lightheaded. What just happened?

'Hello Thaddeus – how was the skirmish?' said Russell, in character. He looked fantastic in his full costume and was relaxing by the fire pit with a pewter tankard of beer, he had been joined by a character in the flowing robes of Urizen. Gwin had no recollection of what Russell's character's name was.

'Hi, er hello. Er…greetings er…Brother.'

'Apparently the Exarch wants to see you, he sent a message.'

Gwin was already unzipping her tent as he spoke. 'Thank you for letting me know, I've just got to get my breath back. Exciting skirmish. Killed some Druj.'

'That's good!' said Russell-in-character. 'Fewer Druj the better.'

Gwin was already in the bell tent. She zipped the door closed and sat on the yielding nylon of her camp bed, her head between her knees. All she could think of was finding the armourer and shaking him firmly by the throat. She'd been taken on adventures before, but this was a whole new level. She needed to lie down for a moment, just a few minutes to collect her thoughts. She swivelled onto the camp bed and closed her eyes.

III

'Come with me,' said the Exarch and led the way through the chapterhouse to the foot of a stairway that spiralled up one of the slim towers. Both men were young, they looked at each other and grinned and then raced one and other up the dozens of tightly turning stairs, to burst out on to the balcony of the tower gasping for breath. The Exarch bent, laughing and panting, his hands on his thighs, Thaddeus leant on the parapet, head between his arms.

It took a few moments to regain their composure, then they stood, looking out over the White City, its spires, belfries, and domes, the pale stone catching pinks and golds from the evening sun. Parts of the city were old, others ancient. Some, like the tower they were standing on, were new, crisp and sharp, their stone bright white, not yet blurred at the edges and mellowed to soft grey by time and the elements.

The Exarch held out his arms as if to embrace the city. He shook his head with wonder and admiration. 'Before humans came this was just wilderness Thaddeus, wilds, woods and marshes, unpopulated except for a few orcs living out their squalid lives, barely different from the animals around them. Humans moved them on and built all this…'

'Drove them off, killed them or enslaved them, as I recall.'

The Exarch frowned, irritated by the interruption. 'Those were less enlightened times.' He returned to his theme. 'Look my friend, just *look* – where there were tangled thickets, now there are streets, where there were muddy ponds, now fountains and tiled pools. It's magnificent, a wonder!'

'Yes, it's a fine city, we can be proud,' said Thaddeus who, in his heart-of-hearts was already itching to return to his company of soldiers and their neat line of tents, his real home, whatever battlefront they happened to be on, and wherever they might be pitched.

'Of course we can!' cried the Exarch. 'Human destiny my friend, human destiny!'

The two men stood for a while admiring the view. A flock of pigeons wheeled among the spires, Thaddeus shaded his eyes and spotted a speck hovering still above them. The hawk, for that was what it was, dived, speeding towards the flock. There was a puff of feathers as it struck and gripped.

'There are seven Virtues,' said the Exarch suddenly. 'Ambition, Courage, Loyalty, Pride…

Prosperity, Vigilance, Wisdom.' Thaddeus completed the catechism, automatically, without thinking.

'Do you recall – as children – how we used to recite the virtues before we were allowed to eat? After we had shown clean hands of course! If you got it wrong, you went to the back of the queue.'

'If you were lucky.'

'Spare the rod and spoil the child.'

'Easy for you to say, you never got much rod.'

'You always struggled, didn't you?'

Thaddeus nodded. 'Yes. I still do, truth be told. None of it ever made as much sense to me as it seemed to make to you. That's why I always let you do the thinking.'

'The Sevenfold Way underpins everything Thaddeus. It is the foundation of our culture, our civilisation; it binds the Empire and is our hope for our eternal souls.'

Thaddeus nodded.

'But,' said the Exarch, 'travel the Empire – and I have – and most citizens struggle to name more than three Virtues and cast about to remember the rest. It's shameful. That ignorance leaves gaps, and gaps become questions, and questions demand answers. And people find answers – the wrong answers.'

'You mean heresy?' said Thaddeus.

The Exarch was still looking out over the city. His slight frame looked sharp, his profile chiselled, hawkish.

'None of the Virtues is more important than the other – we really should write them in a circle, rather than a list – I have written a meditation on the subject.' He digressed, then returned to his point. 'But each of us may have a dedication. Mine is Ambition, yours is Loyalty, is it not?'

'You know it is.'

'It must have been very difficult for you to break your chapter oaths and join me in the new chapter.'

'No, it was not.'

'Then your Loyalty must be a small thing.'

'It is a big thing, but very sharply directed,' said Thaddeus stiffly.

The Exarch looked at Thaddeus, then burst out laughing, punching his shoulder. 'Word games my dear friend. The sort of exercise I do with our visiting scholars and pilgrims.'

'The hours must just fly by.'

The Exarch shook his head. 'Oh Thaddeus.'

'Actually, I have been thinking on the Virtues.'

'Really? That is encouraging.'

Thaddeus blushed and cleared his throat. 'On…On the battlefield, Courage is of great importance – but sometimes people have too much, they become foolhardy, a danger to themselves and others. Exarch, what happens when you have too much of one of the Virtues? What happens when Courage becomes bravado? When does Pride become arrogance? When does Vigilance become paranoia?'

The Exarch groaned and leant his elbows on the parapet, his face in his hands. 'It is just as well that you ask this to me, and here, when there are just the two of us, at the top of this tower, or else you might end up facing an inquisition.' He paused to collect his thoughts, and to try to find a simple explanation that Thaddeus could grasp. 'The Virtues are pure and whole. Courage is not the same thing as bravado. If you are displaying bravado, then that is not Virtuous Courage. You are not being Virtuous.'

'So, you can never have too much Virtue?'

'Of course not! You can only be more Virtuous – so long as you keep to the path, the Sevenfold Way.'

Thaddeus looked out over the city. 'I see.'

The Exarch regarded him for a moment. 'Thaddeus, I don't want you to take offence, because you are a dear and trusted friend, but you have just demonstrated what it is that worries me about the Empire. We must return to a simple, straightforward, muscular, faith. One that leaves no room for doubt or confusion. There is too much discussion Thaddeus, too much wondering. People need someone to tell them what to believe and how to believe. And make certain they do it correctly. The Empire is crying out for leadership Thaddeus – political leadership, religious leadership, and moral leadership. I fear that we stand on a precipice.' The Exarch looked out at the White City. 'I fear all this may revert to forest and swamps and fall in ruins. I really do.'

They stood in silence for a while. Thaddeus spoke, looking out over the city, without turning. 'Are you going to tell me why you summoned me?'

There was a pause.

'I need you to find a moneylender.'

'In the White City?' said Thaddeus, perplexed. 'That will be quite a challenge. I'm not sure Highborn law even permits such a thing.'

'No, in Holberg.'

'Holberg?' Thaddeus was astonished. 'Well, that should be easier, you probably can't throw a stick anywhere in the League without hitting one…But why me? Surely you have the best knowledge of Holberg – you're there all the time?'

'Yes, I'm quite well known there, and my engagement to a member of the late Empress's household is well known too, which is precisely why I can't go around the city knocking on doors looking for a moneylender.'

'I see. As you pointed out, I'm rather stupid – isn't there someone better qualified you could send?'

'Thaddeus, no one has ever accused you of being stupid, you just have a rather shaky grasp of religion, and that, as we both know, is because you choose not to invest time in things that don't interest you.' The Exarch shook his head. 'I fear for your soul my friend, I really do.'

'Any moneylender, or do you have a particular one in mind?'

The Exarch looked at Thaddeus sharply, eyes narrowed, then relaxed into a smile. 'There *is* one in particular.'

'And when I find this person?'

'You borrow some money, quite a lot of money. It is important you understand that the mission I am asking you to undertake does not exist. Nor will it ever exist.'

Gwin saw, through Thaddeus's eyes, the hawk, climbing heavily away, its talons gripping its dead prey. 'I understand,' he said.

'There is a Leaguer, a bishop, who has left Tassato and settled in Holberg. You need to find him.'

'A bishop?'

'Their term – a sort of priest. His name is Rodrigo. A man who has amassed a considerable fortune through careful…investments. He has, I believe, an unrivalled network of contacts – although he might describe them as his "congregation". He has come from nothing, sprung from nowhere, and is regarded as…pragmatic, even by the standards of the League. He may have left Tassato under something of a cloud.'

'Is this the sort of person we want to treat with?'

'Yes, I believe he is. Someone unencumbered by sentiment, prejudice – morality even. In many ways, a most straightforward individual to deal with.'

'And we are going to ask him for a favour?'

'No. You are going to persuade him to make an investment. You will offer him an opportunity, which, I believe, he will find attractive.'

'Which is?'

'To invest in our chapter, and to support my candidacy for the Throne Imperial.'

Thaddeus stared at the Exarch. 'I see. And for us?'

'We will gain something this new chapter of ours is lacking – money Thaddeus. We are growing too slowly, and we are too dependent on the benevolence of the established chapters. We need our independence if we are to move forward.' The Exarch stared out over the White City. 'We will also gain Rodrigo's support, in all manner of useful ways that might be outside of the resources available to a conventional Throne candidate.' He sighed. 'I am determined to save this Empire of ours, but to do so will require commitment, single-mindedness. I must carry the people with me, without getting trapped by their endless bickering, their pettiness, their ignorance, their sentimentality, and their lack of vision.'

He reached into his robe and pulled out some folded parchment. 'You will show Rodrigo these. They are the projected revenues from pilgrims and visiting scholars once we have completed the visitor accommodation. We are attracting more scholars and pilgrims every day, presently they are lodging all over the city. We can spare them the burden of seeking lodgings and increase the valuable time we can spend engaging with them and sharing my…our vision of the Empire renewed.'

'And the candidacy. That is certainly Ambitious.'

'Yes, I am merely a young outsider with no record. It will require funds to campaign. There will be wheels to oil too.'

'And if they don't respond to oil?'

'Then it may be necessary to fall back on the bishop's other resources.'

'I see. I take it you have not discussed this with the chapter founders? This has not been raised at a meeting of the chapel?'

'I feel it would be wisest not to burden them at this point. They can quite easily become confused.'

IV

Thaddeus was back from the White City, back with his company. He wanted to impose his will on the troops, get them used to the change in leadership, and the last thing he needed was a trip to Holberg to intrigue with a Leaguer. Lazarus's departure seemed not to worry the Exarch, who appeared unsurprised, but he gave Thaddeus permission to get his company organised before going to Holberg. What was required was some fighting to get everyone used to the new arrangements – he'd had to appoint his own second-in-command, and that had a knock-on effect all the way through the chain of command. He cursed. Why on earth had Lazarus decided to deploy to Therunin? The whole point of having an independent company was that you could go wherever the fancy and the fighting took you – or avoid fighting altogether, if that's what you preferred, and provide security for merchants and caravans, or even take paid work in the fields, if you so chose.

In truth, Thaddeus knew why: Lazarus had been supporting the Highborn army, being Loyal, because Therunin was an ugly, messy campaign, and it was important to the Highborn because it was in a territory that touched Highguard's southern border. It was an insurgency of briars, humans infected by the magic of the Spring Realm, who were helping to unleash ancient primal forces that threatened to cover the territory with wild and dangerous magical forest, forest that protected itself from fire and axe and infected everything within it. Sometimes, Thaddeus reflected, you just needed a straightforward territorial campaign with barbarian orcs, rather than weird plant-animal, living-dead creatures risen from poisonous greenery and stagnant pools. He understood the importance of securing Highguard's southern border, but he was quite content to leave it to the army. Loyal or not, Thaddeus was taking his troops out of Therunin as soon as possible, not least, because he could not afford to lose any more soldiers to the poisonous air and the contagion of green lung.

Thaddeus had persuaded the general to let him take the company on an extended patrol; light scales of equipment, fast moving, sleeping in their cloaks, a shake down. Minus a standing guard left back at the camp with the administrative staff, and less his sick and wounded, he was down to just over a hundred and thirty effective fighters. Now he stood in the middle of an overgrown cart track, watching carefully as his soldiers passed on either side of him, moving in file, following the ruts on both sides of the track, with skirmishers deployed on the flanks and scouts to the front. He was looking for slackness, a lack of concentration or commitment, but didn't see any. It was a good company, and it seemed they accepted him as their commander without question, despite the fact that he was half Lazarus's age. Lazarus had been right – again. Thaddeus missed him.

A scout ran up, an "unconquered", a bearded Highborn skirmisher in practical green, with light leather armour that made no sound. He was wearing a hooded cloak and carrying a short sword, knife and bow, with a quiver full of arrows and a leather haversack over his shoulder. He stood and saluted, head bowed, clenched fist to his chest. Lazarus had always been strict about discipline, cleanliness, bearing, saluting. The troops grumbled but felt proud and had only contempt for what they regarded as lesser, slack and slovenly companies. 'Commander, there's a village up ahead,' reported the scout.

'Occupied?'

'Yes, but nothing living.'

Welcome to Therunin, thought Thaddeus. He raised his eyebrows. 'What are we looking at?'

'Husks.'

'Right, show me.'

The company halted well back under the file leaders. Thaddeus went forward until he was met by the scouts, who were watching a clearing from the edge of the woods. It was dense foliage, secondary growth where fields were returning to nature, and no sign of grazing by deer or other animals. There was indeed a village, wildly and frighteningly overgrown, but with a scatter of figures slowly moving around: the dead population still inhabiting their rotting homesteads and collapsed cottages. 'Any surprises?' Thaddeus asked. 'Have you been right around?'

The lead scout nodded; she scratched a map on the ground with her dagger. 'The road goesss ssstraight through, though it'sss even more overgrown on the other sside. The husksss are all in among the housesss.' Sister Marah spoke with a sibilant hiss; she was lineaged and heavily so, a naga, a human touched – the Highborn might say contaminated – by the magical Night Realm. The skin of her upper face had hardened into scales, and there were feathers at the edge of her hairline and at her temples. Her eyes were yellow, with slit pupils, when she spoke Thaddeus could see her prominent, pointed upper canine teeth. Life wasn't easy for her back in Highguard, she was happier soldiering. Marah was unusually hardy for a naga, and Thaddeus had never encountered a more skilled infiltrator.

Thaddeus thought for a minute. 'I want the scouts as a stop party on the far side. I'll need the company brought up, we'll deploy along this edge, advance through, cut down everything that moves and burn the place.' He turned to the scout who had brought him forward. 'Go back and get me the file leaders.'

As a soldier, Thaddeus had seen more than his share of death, but the dead still revolted him. He always thought how dishevelled dead animals looked, their fur or feathers in disarray. Dead people were worse, falling into strange positions they would never have formed in life, and repulsive as they decayed. The husks were dead people overtaken by animated plant forms that grew in and through their bodies, the bodies were most certainly dead, but the plants were not. The husks mostly stood about in the sun, or near water, but if threatened, would become wildly dangerous, and were quite difficult to destroy. However, Thaddeus's company was making a thorough job of it, overwhelming the relatively few husks in the village and hacking them to pieces. Some soldiers were digging into thatched rooves with their swords, to find dry straw under the sodden outer layers, then setting it alight with flint-and-steel. Smoke billowed into the air and sparks and embers spiralled upwards as roof beams collapsed and the wrecked buildings blazed and fell in on themselves.

Thaddeus stood watching the troops, knowing he cut a fine, commanding figure. The new greaves and vambraces were comfortable, a perfect fit, and worth the considerable extra expense. It was just as well they were such a good fit, considering all the walking the company had done. Suddenly Thaddeus felt something collide with his right leg and looked down – an ettercap, a distorted, hugely enlarged insect had its mandibles wrapped around his steel-clad leg. He looked at it with disgust, a beetle, but about the size of a small dog. At this scale, you could see all the furry bits and other details that were mercifully invisible in its smaller cousins. Thaddeus brought his sword down on it, but the point slid off the creature's carapace. He took more careful aim, put the point in the joint of its back, and was about to push the blade home when he changed his mind. He struggled to disengage himself from the ettercap, twisting and shaking his leg free and conscious that his fine commanding figure was somewhat diminished wrestling with a two-foot-tall cockroach. He shook the thing off and poked it with his sword until it scuttled away. Why had he done that? He wondered. It would have been quicker and easier just to kill the revolting thing. Somewhere inside his conscience something was telling him that even ettercaps had a right to live, and this was their forest, not his. He shook his head; he was going soft. Thaddeus wiped his sword blade with a handful of grass. He sighed. It wasn't a proper battle, but it was the best they were going to get, and they were going to make sure no one was in any doubt they had passed that way and left their mark. Slash and burn. Doing the Empire's work. And that made it alright, didn't it? Whatever.

They were a good company, he thought. *His* good company.

Flames from the chapter fire pit were lighting the roof of the tent with flickering orange light. The nylon and spring steel camp bed gave a protesting groan. It was rated ninety-five kilos, which should have given Gwin a very comfortable margin, but, she realised, she was still in armour and chainmail and the ironmongery, chiefly the mail, was extremely heavy. She gingerly rolled off the bed onto the groundsheet floor of the tent, clambered to her feet, unfastened and removed her vambraces and greaves, mostly working by feel, and then, bent almost double, sloughed-off the tightly fitting chainmail hauberk, wriggling and shaking herself out of it, exactly like some marginal illustration in the Morgan Bible or the Bayeux Tapestry. She could almost feel her body expanding and breathing as the metal came off. Had she really slept in her armour?

She guessed by the voices outside the tent it was time-out – happy campers, not in-character conversation. That made it 1am on Saturday morning. She probably ought to go out and see how everyone else was doing, but her mind was spinning and reeling. Gwin peeled off the rest of her kit, using up what energy she had left. Standing, she struggled into her sleeping bag, pulling it on like clothes, then hopped and wriggled back to the camp bed, lay down and pulled her faux fur blanket over and puffed up her pillow. She looked up at the roof of the tent, the voices were diminishing, the fire was dying down, everyone was going to bed.

The camp was asleep, the tired soldiers relieved to be safe, clean, and fed, and back under canvas. Thaddeus was in his tent, packing up his travelling kit and hanging it on his furca, the T-shaped pole that soldiers shouldered on the march. His bedroll, his haversack with spare clothing and washing and shaving kit, eating utensils. He would be travelling light, without the benefit of the company's baggage carts, but without armour and a slung shield he would make quick time. He had completed his paperwork and handed over the troops to his second-in-command, and the administration of the camp to his camp prefect. He stretched, noted how much his muscles ached and decided it was time for a steam bath in the wood-and-canvas lodge his soldiers had built. If the fire wasn't still lit, and the stones hot, he would be seriously displeased.

Thaddeus saw his sword lying on his camp cot and cursed, took it up, and found his whetstone, rags, and the bottle of kraken oil he had brought back from Sermersuaq. Now *that* had been a proper fight. The Jotun were civilised for barbarian orcs, more civilised than a few Imperials Thaddeus could name. It had been cold though, as Guardian Lazarus had said – "proper cold". Blood in the snow, a battle on the ice of a frozen lake. Happy days. Thaddeus shook his head, unsheathed the sword and wiped the blade with an oily rag, several wipes, hilt to tip, never the other way, then the same with a clean dry rag. Then he started to give each edge a series of long smooth strokes with the whetstone. He felt the edges with his thumb, then tried them against the hairs on his arm – sharp enough. He wiped the blade again and lightly oiled it, then pulled the sheath onto the blade. While he was at it, he took his greaves and vambraces from the armour stand, put a little oil and rottenstone on the metal of each item, rubbed it off the surface, then oiled the armour. He put it back on the stand – at least it wouldn't be rusty when he got back. Time to bathe. At last.

There was a lamp by the lodge, Thaddeus guessed the fire was still lit. As he approached a small figure detached itself from the dark silhouette of the company bathhouse.

'Hello Barnabas,' said Thaddeus, 'What are you doing still up?'

The boy was from one of the families who followed the company rather than staying back at the chapterhouse. It was uncomfortable and dangerous, but it meant they stayed together, and they provided useful help and support around camp. Barnabas was in a belted tunic and had wrapped a blanket around his shoulders against the cold night air.

'Kept the fire going for you sir.'

'Thank you. When are you becoming a squire, you must be almost ten?'

'In the autumn sir. Can't wait!'

'Yes, you'll love it. It'll probably be a rest camp compared to being with us. We'll miss you though.'

'I want to join the company when I've done my service. If you'll have me sir.'

'I'll want to hear the reason if you don't join us!' Thaddeus smiled. 'Goodness, going up in the autumn? I remember…I remember when the Exarch and I weren't much more than your age, snotty-nosed new squires doing all the jobs no one else wanted. He hated pulling the naga skins out of the sump in the baths.'

The boy shrugged. 'I've done worse.'

'That's the spirit. It's all just a game, always remember that.'

It was morning, and Gwin was looking up at the brightly sunlit roof of a bell tent. Waking up and wondering where you are is a condition that afflicts many busy people but waking up wondering *who* you are is a little more unusual. Since she had been skittled over by a picture vehicle, a vintage truck, in an on-set accident, it had become something of a feature of Gwin's life. She lay still and listened. No rumble of artillery that narrowed the field. She looked across the tent for someone who, had he ever existed, would have been considerably more than a century old. She felt a pang of loss and sadness. Instead of another cot and the sleeping form of a young officer, there was a pile of reusable supermarket bags full of assorted clothing and bits, her backpack, makeup bag, and some fruit and Haribos. Suddenly she needed Starmix gummies more than life itself.

For the briefest moment, Gwin entertained the grim possibility of slogging over to queue for the showers in the out-of-character area, but then remembered with relief that the good Lord had, in his infinite wisdom, provided grateful humankind with baby wipes. She struggled out of her sleeping bag, found them in a side pocket of her backpack and thoroughly freshened-up to face whatever a new and full day of larp might bring. She re-applied underarm roll-on and shoved the handful of used wipes into her bin liner rubbish bag, along with three empty Starmix mini bags. As the plastic bag opened, there was a brief waft of decay from an apple core and some tangerine peel, and she remembered the ruined village and shuddered, she'd never look at her house plants in quite the same way again.

So now it was Day Two, and time-in was at ten. Friday had only been 6 pm to 1 in the morning, there was still all of

Saturday and most of Sunday to go. Beth always took the Monday after a larp event as leave – which Gwin had previously considered pretty wet. Now, *bloody hell!* She was going to need a week off in a darkened room if Friday was anything to go by.

There was chatter and laughter outside, as players woken early by the bright morning sun rubbed sleepy eyes, pondered breakfast, and gathered to discuss the first few hours of the event. Gwin emerged from her tent in her Xavier Institute varsity top, leggings, and wellies, with a toothbrush in her mouth and a bottle of water in her hand, to discover a small crowd of off duty larpers had gathered on and around the benches and trestle table. Russell and another were smokily attempting to get the fire pit relit. After several hours of occupying their characters, everyone was determinedly being themselves, whatever that might mean. In Russell's case, he was wearing a dangerously stretched grey and white rabbit onesie, open to the waist to reveal a faded Mandalorian T-shirt, which was riding up to expose an ample and hairy belly. He had the rabbit's hood and ears up, but the effect was more Donnie Darko than Beatrix Potter. Beth was in cut-off jeans, yellow crocks and a brown dressing gown styled like a Jedi robe; she was eating instant porridge out of its pot.

Gwin toyed with the idea of doing the old film crew trick of pouring milk straight into a variety pack Coco Pops, and then eating them out of the box, which always attracted comment, and then decided that even the precious single box of chocolaty cereal in the variety pack in her tent just wasn't going to cut it today, and something much more substantial was required this breakfast time. Her mouth felt fur lined, and she scrubbed her teeth, rinsed with cold bottled water, then spat in the grass behind her tent.

'You have to tell us about the skirmish,' said Beth. 'What on earth happened? There was a whole posse of Dawnish looking for you last night. We didn't know where you had gone.'

'Bit of a fatigue crash afterwards,' said Gwin. 'All this takes a bit of getting used to. There's so much to remember and understand.' She thought for a moment, remembering the carvings on the Sentinel Gate – rearing Imperial horses, held with real chains. 'Like horses, for example.'

'Horses?' said Beth, blankly.

'Yes, how does everyone get around? There aren't any horses.'

'The horses died out long ago, they're almost legendary,' explained Russell, 'which also stops anyone being tempted to bring a real one along to an event.'

'But there are oxes? I read that on the wiki or something.'

'Oxen, yes.'

'Are they like, flying ones, like flying bison?'

'Like Appa?'

'Yes.'

'No. They are the ordinary kind.'

'It must take ages to get anywhere.'

'The roads, the trods, are magic.'

Gwin thought about it. 'Like those walkways you get at airports?'

'Pretty much,' said Beth.

'Makes sense,' said Gwin, whose capacity to accept the peculiar was always fairly broad.

'It's more…more like the trods are magical and stop travellers being exhausted by their journey,' said Russell.

'In exactly the way the M25 doesn't?' said Gwin.

'There are Imperial Highways and Red Roads too, and mundane roads, but as a rule it doesn't take more than a fortnight to get anywhere in the Empire.'

'Just like the M25 then. Pity though, about the horses, I mean.'

'Do you ride?'

'I military ride, I can use a sword or lance on a horse. It must affect the hierarchy of the Empire too.'

'How so?' asked Beth.

'Well,' said Gwin, slipping into a groove, 'in all medieval European societies the ruling class were the equestrian class, the word for knight is the word for 'rider' in most languages except English: *ridder*, *ritter*, *caballero*, *chevalier*. They're the lowest order of nobility, the *equites*, the horsed class, the next one down from the senatorial class in ancient Rome.'

'Why is English different?' asked Russell.

'English is different because knight comes from the Anglo-Saxon *cniht*, which means servant – so part of a noble's household.'

'Sorry,' said Beth, 'she gets like this.'

Russell was quite enjoying the rabbit hole. 'The Empire's not a true democracy, but it is a meritocracy, so anyone can get to be anything, including a knight, if you're Dawnish. There's voting, but it's in voting colleges like the Senate for senators, Conclave for mages, the Synod for priests…'

The female player who played the Exarch joined them and squeezed onto the bench by the trestle table. She was wearing a pink hoodie and the exarch's black riding boots over cat-patterned pyjama bottoms. She pulled a banana out of the pocket at the front of the hoodie, peeled it, broke off a section and popped it in her mouth. After a couple of chews, she said 'What happened at the skirmish? Apparently, the Dawnish want to make you a knight or something. Or give you a flower. Or both maybe.'

'Their flowers mean things,' said Beth, 'You'd better watch out for that.'

It was seeing the Exarch's boots that did it. Gwin groaned and put her face in her hands. 'Are you okay?' asked Beth, looking concerned.

'Immersion sickness.'

'*What*?'

'Immersion sickness. This going in and out of character is totally doing my head in.'

'*Immersion sickness*!' said Russell. 'I love that, I'm going to steal it!'

'Steal away. I have got to get some breakfast.'

'Vegan, veggie, or carnivore?' Russell asked.

'Sizzling bacon! I always say it helps to start the day with something greasy inside you.'

'I wish you would stop staying that,' said Beth.

'Sorry, I've been keeping bad company.'

In her mind, Gwin heard the voice of the officers' mess cook a long, long time ago, on a battlefield far away, and her mind's eye saw him swelling with pride when she called him "chef". She saw herself accepting a proffered gift of sandwiches wrapped in newspaper, and a bottle of cold tea. And she saw mud and barbed wire, and she felt that empty ache of loss...

Someone was saying something. Gwin pulled herself together.

'They do bacon rolls down there,' said a player called Baz, who was holding a Moomin plushie and had very short, dyed orange hair.

'You mean the place at the end that does the drink refills?'

'That's the one.'

'I'm off. See you all later…'

'Don't forget we've got to get kitted-up for the battle!' Baz called after her.

Gwin finished off the last mouthful of bacon roll and licked ketchup off her fingers.

'We still haven't heard how your first larp experience went,' said Beth. 'You dressed up, went off on a skirmish and disappeared. I guess the fact you're still here is a good sign.'

Gwin paused to consider. 'It was *so* hard to get into character. I just totally felt like I was in fancy dress. Until we crossed through the Sentinel Gate – then it got pretty real.'

'I think everyone starts off just playing themselves,' said Beth.

'Themselves, but the bad version!' said Russell.

Everybody pondered for a bit. 'I'm not sure that's true,' said Gwin, 'surely not everyone is bad. Thaddeus isn't…'

'Unless you're an orc!' said Beth. 'I heard about the skirmish!'

'It was them or us,' said Gwin. 'I don't think it was personal. Actually, I think Thaddeus quite respects orcs and feels a bit sorry for them.'

'And that,' said Beth, 'is your character already developing.'

'Yes, I understand what you mean.' Gwin looked about. 'Where's Baz?'

'They've gone off to get kitted up.'

'Er…Baz's character is a battle mage, right?'

'Yes, so leather mage armour and a staff, and quite useful if you get injured.'

'And the Exarch?'

'Also getting kitted up, but for meetings, not for battle.'

'I love the way everyone is doing different things.'

'People get different things out the event,' said Russell. He poked the fire pit. 'Some just want to sit by the fire and do a bit around camp, some want to do back-to-back skirmishes and battles, some want to sell stuff, and some want the shenanigans.'

'The lure of the hat,' said Beth.

Gwin was confused. 'The *what*?'

'Hats are Imperial posts. They go from really minor sinecures to being a senator or cardinal or arch-mage or general, and really affecting Imperial policy. Of course, you've got to get people to vote for you. You can even go right to the top and be Emperor or Empress, seeing as we currently have a vacancy on the Throne.'

'Winning friends and influencing people?'

'Or bullying, blackmailing and bribing them,' put in Russell, gleefully.

'Crime happens?'

Russell nodded. 'Conspiracy is a big thing – coming in as plot, from the game-makers, or from the players themselves. And there have been some absolutely epic frauds. There are also religious and magical crimes – heretics can be executed, and that has happened. A lot of people who come from D and

D start off wanting to be thieves and pickpockets like they would be in Dungeons and Dragons, but it's complicated in live role play, because someone is really going to take exception if you go into their tent and start helping yourself to their kit, or if you cut the strings on their handmade leather purse. It can be done, and the stuff taken generally has to go straight to GOD, but it's complicated and there's quite a few rules. It's one of those things that doesn't come over easily from playing D and D. Larp operates differently really.' Russell put another log on the fire.

Beth said, 'Murder happens, but it's really discouraged – otherwise Anvil would be waist-deep in bodies. Murderers get hunted down by the militia, tried and punished…'

'If they catch them,' said Russell.

'True,' said Beth.

'And the battlefield can be a dangerous place,' said Russell, archly, 'if you've made enemies on your own side. Unfortunate accidents can happen in the confusion – stories abound.'

Gwin shook her head. 'There's rather a lot more to this than just loads of people in a field hitting each other with rubber swords.'

'Yes, and there is that too. Talking of which, you need to get ready. Do you need help?'

'The tape's still on.'

'How's that working?'

'Good, or so far so good. If I was in a binder, I'd be climbing the walls by now. Honestly, I sometimes wish they could just unscrew or something.'

'Hair and makeup?'

'I'm going to go a bit easier than I did yesterday, a lot of that was nerves, and I think I can pull off Thaddeus's body language and manner better now.'

V

Over three hundred players from five of the Empire's ten nations were gathering by the Sentinel Gate, for the Saturday morning battle, while the same number from the remaining nations were down at the bottom of the out-of-character area, putting on makeup and orc masks and collecting arms and armour to play the Druj enemy. Massed, fully costumed and ready for battle, the players were an extraordinary sight, and even for someone who had done her share of epic films; Gwin thought there seemed to be an awful lot of them. And there was music. Recorded music was banned on the site, but a female choir was singing the Imperial battle anthem *a cappella*, and the clear sharp voices over the hubbub of the gathering soldiery made the hairs on Gwin's arms stand up.

She suddenly found herself wondering if Thaddeus was experiencing Gwin, the way Gwin was experiencing Thaddeus. That was a disconcerting thought. She stood quietly for a minute, casting about in her mind in case there was a stowaway on board, but, rather to her relief, there was nothing. Thaddeus was, though, much more real to her now than he had been when she created him in her Empire player account. She might not *be* Thaddeus, but she could do a good impression, and she did, carrying herself like the Highborn he was.

Generals were haranguing their contingents, and one or other group of soldiers would suddenly burst into a cheer. The Highborn were kneeling, blocks of chapters visible from the different colours and sigils of their surcoats, receiving a benediction from a rather long-winded priest. Gwin channelled her inner-Thaddeus and ignored all that. Near the Sentinel Gate end of the Highguard camp stood two figures, a mother and daughter. The little girl was holding a bowl of water, the mother a leafy branch. Gwin knew immediately what Thaddeus would do. She approached the two and took a knee, head bowed, sword drawn, point down in the ground, hands resting on the hilt. There was stillness, in Gwin's mind the sounds of the soldiers and the choir faded. The mother dipped the twigs in the water and, in benediction, flicked it over the kneeling Gwin-as-Thaddeus, who remained still a moment, eyes closed, then stood, thanked them with a nodding bow, and turned and joined the throng of warriors waiting to charge through the Sentinel Gate. Gwin took Thaddeus's accustomed place at the front, shrugged to ease the weight of the mail hauberk on sore shoulders, slipped her arm through the leather loop on the shield and grabbed the grip, then she drew her shortsword.

The Highguard contingent were the last to join the throng at the gate, unhurriedly going straight to the front. This was not, it turned out, due to any deference, but rather sheer practicality. There were fifteen or more cataphracts, covered head-to-toe in massive plate armour, and even more guardians, like Thaddeus, with mail hauberks and plate vambraces and greaves, all carrying shields. No one was quite sure what they would find on the other side of the gate, and the heavy infantry of Highguard would go through like a battering ram, clearing the way for the soldiers of the other nations to follow.

'Have you got anti-venom?'

Gwin-as-Thaddeus looked around to find Baz-in-character, in a long robe, with elaborately tooled leather vambraces on their arms, pauldrons on their shoulders and wide hero belt. 'Er…no,' said Gwin-as-Thaddeus.

Baz's character rummaged in a pouch and pulled out a tiny bottle and a card. 'If you need to, drink this.'

'Thank you.' Gwin knew from the briefing on Friday she would also have to tear the card in half once she had used the anti-venom. It could literally be a lifesaver though, as otherwise Druj poison on blade and bolt would ensure she bled out faster than aid could reach her, like the unfortunate Marcher on the skirmish. She carefully put the bottle and card in her pouch.

They advanced through the grey stone arch of the Sentinel Gate, and Gwin tried to determine the moment when the transformation happened. It was lost in the hurly-burly as hundreds of players pushed through, but suddenly, through a slight shimmer, she found herself once again a consciousness floating in the mind of a young male warrior, in a real army, on a real battlefield.

Gwin picked up Thaddeus's irritation. He was used to command; it had been a while since he had been a common foot soldier, and he disliked these Imperial hero battles. Some of the fighters were the finest in the Empire, some thought they were, and some hoped to be. Whom you were standing alongside was potluck. Thaddeus longed for the two hundred spears of his company – *his* company, that had a good ring to it – but his Loyalty prevailed. Steadiness and discipline were what the Imperial soldiers were going to need in this battle. Unlike the heroic Jotun or the buccaneering Grendel, both orc nations the Empire was generally at war with, the vicious Druj were the orcs of nightmare. The whole horizon seemed to be filled with a shrieking, yelling mass of ragged, painted orcs, clothed in misty shades of green and grey splashed with acid greens and yellows and blood reds. Above them waved tattered banners thick with crusted blood, hung with skulls, bones, rotting body parts, and scalps. Behind them, yellow smoke rose from fires where their shamans danced and cursed, and to the front and above their heads waved a forest of jagged blades.

The left of the Imperial line was made up of Highborn cataphracts and guardians, with sword and shield. Behind them was a rank of League pole arms – pikes and spears, halberds and glaives. They were opposed by lightly equipped, fast-moving Druj, who would rush in, swinging long poleaxes and flails and jabbing with spears, trying to get under the shields to stab at thighs and shins with filthy or poisoned blades, and, if lucky, hamstring an Imperial. Thaddeus felt a blade grate on the steel of his greves. He stepped towards his attacker, inside the reach of the orc's long-bladed bill and held off the next orc with his shield while he skewered his attacker on the shortsword. The whole Imperial line started to move forward, catching the orcs by surprise, the Druj rear ranks still pushing forward as the front rank tried to fall back.

This was the point when those with polearms needed to shorten their grip – but to do so took training and discipline, which were not Druj characteristics. Also, this was the point when each soldier in the line had to depend on the shield of their comrade to the right, and in turn defend the soldier to their left, which was exactly what the Highborn had been trained to do. The front row of orcs was crushed between Highborn and their own still-advancing rear ranks, their polearms lost in the advancing ranks of Imperials, and no longer giving any advantage. This was what Thaddeus carried a short sword for, and it jabbed in and out of the mass of orcs, the dead piling up before him. Thaddeus wasn't alone, the cataphract to his right grinned at him over her shield. They were going to win, and they knew it. They were the anvil of Empire, the rock against which the waves of enemy would break.

To the right another powerful block, fronted by round-shielded Wintermarkers, the famed Green Shields, were fighting in their own way, axes rising and falling, cleaving orcs, pushing them back in the same way as the Highborn and their comrades from the League, were on the left flank. Between the two were a mass of crossbows and archers, and it was here that the Druj suddenly pushed forward. The lightly armed centre bowed, broke, and collapsed, and suddenly there were three battles, with the Imperials in the ascendant on the flanks and a rout in the centre, with screaming Druj pouring through to surround the flanks and attack them from the rear.

Thaddeus and the Highborn alongside him were unaware of the disaster unfolding, still confidently slaughtering the Druj to their front.

'Can't you...afford...a decent...sword?' teased the tall cataphract, between blows, her long sword cutting down on orc heads, her white-painted armour splashed and streaming with orc blood.

Thaddeus was stabbing with a frightening economy of effort, his wickedly sharp shortsword flicking in and out of the orc ranks. Gwin was uncomfortably aware of how she might put Thaddeus off his stroke, and not at all sure what would happen to them both if Thaddeus fell on this real battlefield to a real orc blade. She stayed as innocuous as she could. At least, she now understood why Thaddeus had such well-developed shoulders.

'I inherited…my…father's…sword!'

'I…thought that…was an…old joke! Surely no…one really…does that!'

'I did.'

'What…happened to…your father?'

'Killed by the…Druj.'

'There's…probably…a…lesson…there…'

Suddenly the pressure eased, and the Druj line thinned and the orcs to their front were able to fall back, standing more than a spear's length away, raging at them, hurling taunts. The Highborn paused to draw breath. A League pikeman with grey steel back and breast, and tassets and plumed kettle hat pushed forward between Thaddeus and the cataphract, grinning at them, and clearing space for one of his colleagues to make certain of the piled orcs lying in blood-soaked heaps around their feet with his war hammer.

'That went well,' said the cataphract. Her face was splashed with Druj blood. Thaddeus noticed she had the stumps of horns on her forehead, a cambion who had cut away those symbols of contamination from the magical realms. Many nations thought nothing of lineage, but magical influence on humans deeply worried the Highborn. Lineage could and did rise to high office – after all there had been lineaged incumbents on the Throne – but in Highguard they were always watched closely: for their own protection, of course. Thaddeus remembered as he approached his teens the fear that lineage might emerge – the lumps of budding horns or antlers, scales, gills even. Luckily, he was pure, unsullied human. He counted himself fortunate.

Suddenly Druj struck the rear of the Imperial line like a tidal wave, and as they did, braying bugles sent those to the front charging back into the fight. The Imperials were fully surrounded, fighting on all sides, with terrified light troops, the crossbows and archers, running for their lives, pursued by shrieking, baying Druj.

The Leaguer turned around to face the new threat from the rear, swinging his pike up between Thaddeus and the cataphract, and they closed towards each other, as did the soldiers on either side of them. The Imperial line began to contract, and then diminish into two irregular islands of frantic fighters in a sea of orcs. Thaddeus stepped backwards, caught his heel on one of the orc bodies and fell amongst the dead. The cataphract made a great horizontal sweep with her long sword to buy them both space and crouched so he could struggle to his feet covered by her shield. An arrow punched her shield, the ugly barbed point fully through the layered wood.

'Are you absolutely determined to follow in your father's footsteps?'

'Not today.'

'Then get up.'

It was difficult for Thaddeus to find his footing in the yielding mass of Druj and Imperial corpses. As he did so, the cataphract was already back in the fight. Except for her head and feet, she was encased in armour, her neck protected by tall *passe gardes* or swordbreakers on the big pauldrons that covered her shoulders. It was an overhand stroke with a heavy bladed bill that landed inside one of these, the ragged blade slicing superficially along the side of her neck, missing the artery, but leaving a long, jagged cut. The cataphract thrust her sword into the orc's mouth and up into the brain, but as the orc fell, she stumbled, then crumpled to the ground.

'Healer!' Thaddeus shouted. He looked about wildly. 'Where's a healer?'

The cataphract had collapsed against a dead Druj, her body was limp, there were shadowy black lines beneath the skin of her neck and face, radiating out from the wound, venom in her bloodstream, there was foam on her lips, she was gasping for breath, eyes wide as she struggled for air. Thaddeus put his sword into his left hand, his shield hanging slack on its arm loop. One-handed, he wrenched open his pouch, tearing at the leather, and found the tiny bottle. He battled to grasp it with the blood-slicked leather fingers of his glove, somehow he pulled it out. He turned to the cataphract. 'Take this!'

She could barely respond. 'No…yours.'

Thaddeus felt a rain of blows on his shield as he pulled the cork out of the tiny bottle with his teeth. He could taste the orc blood on his glove. He stooped and poured the liquid into the cataphract's mouth. Something struck him across the shoulders, he felt the blow, but whatever the blade was, his mail hauberk stopped it, and the padded gambeson beneath absorbed most of the impact. He had done what he could for the cataphract, he took his sword back into his right hand, as he did so, saw a small mage struggling through the twisting, battling bodies, almost on all fours, towards the fallen Highborn in her blood-splashed white armour. There was a huge orc charging towards Thaddeus, disadvantaged, he could only raise his shield to protect himself from the orc's cleaver, and as he did so, the mage pointed towards the orc with their staff and called out some words Thaddeus didn't understand, and suddenly the orc was frozen, his feet seemed to be rooted to the ground, he roared with rage and Thaddeus sprang at him, driving his shortsword into the orc and right through his body. Thaddeus looked back to see the mage squatting beside the cataphract. He smashed his shield into the face of one orc, parried a sword thrust, and drove his sword into another Druj belly.

Suddenly the Druj started to thin out and orcs began running to the right, along the front of the Imperial line. It seemed there had been a plan all along. Imperial light troops – hooded Highborn unconquered, robed Urizeni swordfighters and wild, bounding Freeborn of the Brass Coast, had been moving up through thick cover on the left flank, to swing, like a closing door, to crush the Druj between themselves and the heavily armed line of Imperials already engaged, in a classic hammer-and-anvil manoeuvre. The trouble was, the difficult terrain had slowed the move and by the time the fresh light troops burst out onto the battlefield, the heavy infantry were surrounded and almost overwhelmed, a few sword thrusts from catastrophe. Jotun or even Grendel would have held their line, driven back the skirmishers, and finished off the flagging heavy infantry, handing the Empire a military disaster. But the Druj lacked the taste for that kind of fight. They had lost enough and inflicted enough, and now fled the field, determined to live, and fight another day. There was a raucous cheer from the light troops, but no response from the battered blood-soaked heavies, who knew how close they had come to obliteration.

The Sentinel's Gate was open, and it was time to withdraw. Thaddeus was part of the perimeter of shields that slowly collapsed in towards the gate as the injured, dead and dying were evacuated, and the lighter troops streamed through. He looked over his shoulder at the eerie glow of the portal and thought what an asset it was to the Empire. What must it be like for the Empire's enemies to have that appear, suddenly and at random, and hundreds of Imperial warriors pour through? He had to admit, the Druj had done well to respond as quickly and decisively as they had, and they had come close to inflicting a memorable defeat. It would be hailed as a victory, of course, but as Thaddeus felt the orc blood soaking his right glove and arm slowly congealing, he just felt weary and oddly ashamed. He just wanted to get back to his company, but that wasn't to be. He was on a mission, and as soon as he was clean and rested, he would be back on the trods, heading for the fortress city of Holberg, one of the four independent cities that made up the League.

Gwin made a determined effort to stay on her feet and manage a confident Thaddeus-like Highborn walk – although in truth she just wanted to slump against something solid and throw up. Her female body felt light compared to the male Thaddeus she had been occupying, but she had kept his aching exhaustion. She could barely lift her right arm. Curiously, she was no stranger to close combat, but previously that had been at pistol-range, and the skirmish where she had first encountered the real Thaddeus had had a kind of balletic quality about it. The battle had been something else entirely, and she would never read history in quite the same way again. The press, the closeness, the utter confusion, a massive, heaving, brutal brawl, eye-to-eye, toe-to-toe. Intimate, no-holds-barred, in-your-face, smell-their-breath, taste-their-blood, protracted slaughter. Gwin stood still, trying to slow her breathing, her heart was beating out her chest. Two Highborn pushed past with a cataphract slumped between them, her arms around their shoulders, her feet dragging on the grass. It was her, Thaddeus's battle companion from the shield wall. Well, it wasn't, but it was her player-character version. Her chapter comrades were rushing her into the big green tent of the field hospital.

Around the Sentinel Gate were jubilant boastful heroes, heartbroken grieving mourners, and helpless agonised wounded, dozens of players role-playing their hearts out in noisy chaos. Healers and helpers darted around, and someone offered Gwin-as-Thaddeus a drink from a waterskin. Gwin suddenly realised how desperately thirsty she was and took the waterskin, holding it high, splashing the cold water into her mouth. She wiped her mouth with the back of her hand and handed the skin back. Then she walked over to the hospital. The cataphract player was lying on a bed just inside the entrance of the big tent. Gwin-as-Thaddeus stepped through the throng of groaning wounded and busy healers and knelt by her, taking her hand. The cataphract player gave a weak smile of recognition.

'That was some fight!' said Gwin-as-Thaddeus.

The cataphract player nodded. She was barely able to speak. 'Thank you for saving me.' She gasped.

'Likewise.'

The cataphract player was mouthing something. Gwin-as-Thaddeus put her ear by the cataphract player's mouth. 'My pouch,' the cataphract player murmured.

Gwin looked down, saw the belt pouch and opened it. Inside was a small spritzer bottle. Gwin looked carefully, it was full of stage blood. The cataphract player raised her eyebrows and nodded. Gwin looked around, then spritzed blood over the player's white armour, a little in her face, and then sprayed some over herself. She put the spritzer bottle back in the player's pouch, squeezed her hand, and said, 'I'll see you back in Highguard, Sister.'

VI

Gwin was determined to manage some role play with the chapter when she got back to the tents, she certainly felt she earned it, and she was now dishevelled, sweaty, and heroically splashed with stage blood. She was most disappointed to find the chapter camp empty, with the fire pit burned down to grey ashes. Everyone was out and about, playing full tilt. It suddenly occurred to her that what was missing was somewhere to wash in-character. There should be wash bowls; what was the matter with these people, didn't they read the national brief on the wiki? She made a mental note to bring one for Thaddeus next time she came – which rather suggested she had already decided to come again. Then she remembered there *was* one, a large silver bowl, in the chapter tent. Gwin-as-Thaddeus entered the big seven-metre double bell. Against the back wall was a narrow wallpapering table covered with a damask cloth that spread out on the floor, making an impressive altar. On the altar was a big triptych altarpiece celebrating the founding of the chapter, a mosaic of the Labyrinth of Ages – typical Highborn work – and two tall elaborate brass candlesticks, on top of which fat electric theatre candles flickered. The altar was flanked by the chapter standards.

Gwin noted with a flash of irritation that the altar was also decorated with a greasy paper plate holding a chicken leg bone and half an individual apple pie, as well as a crumpled paper napkin and two empty beer bottles. Her inner Thaddeus fumed. He might not be particularly religious, especially for a Highborn, but he did have respect. She collected the litter, found the rubbish bag, and tipped it in. Fitted between the two poles of the big tent was a long table, surrounded by director's chairs with the chapter sigil embroidered on the back. Here in the chapel was where the senior members of the chapter met to decide chapter policy, chaired by the Exarch. In the centre of the table was the silver wash bowl, standing on three feet, each a mask of a bearded face, it had two elaborate handles, and in the water floated rose petals. Alone, unwatched, Gwin-as-Thaddeus rinsed her fingertip and wiped her hands over her face and over her short hair.

Gwin stood her shield by the door and clambered back into her sun-warmed bell tent. She stiffly removed her armour and sword belt, slipped off her surcoat and started the contortions it took to get the mail hauberk off. She took off her sweat soaked gambeson and kept going: the tape was going to have to come off too before she did herself a mischief. Untaped, baby wiped and clad in clean boxers, Gwin arranged her rolled sleeping bag and her backpack as a bolster, put her pillow on top of it, and leaned back. She decided her medium-term future would involve a bath filled to the overflow, hot as she could bear, and one, possibly two, Lush bath bombs – the ridiculously over-the-top ones she had been saving since Christmas. But Sunday night was still a long way and a lot of larping away. The tent was deliciously warm, it was quiet, and from where she had opened the ventilation flaps at the bottom of the walls came the warm meadow hay smell of the grass. She was so tired.

The Highborn struck an austere figure in the cluttered richness of Bishop Rodrigo's chambers. His plain black travelling habit, with the hood up, looked almost sinister in a riot of reds and golds, velvets and brocades, mirrors and precious metals, which glowed and twinkled in the light of dozens of candles. Thaddeus raised his right hand. 'May the benevolence of the Paragons and the guidance of the Exemplars illuminate the Way for you and speed your Virtuous soul through the Labyrinth of Ages.'

There was an awkward silence, then Bishop Rodrigo di Tassato, sitting on a cushioned throne at the head of a long table laden with food, belched loudly, and said, 'Quite so. I couldn't have put it better myself.'

The Highborn pushed back his hood and regarded Rodrigo. 'Do I have the honour of addressing his Excellency the Bishop Rodrigo Borges Mão de Ferro di Tassato?'

'You do, although your pronunciation is execrable.'

'Forgive me, and please forgive my ignorance of your customs, but should that not be 'van Holberg' if you live in this city?'

The bishop fluttered a hand irritably. 'I regard my presence here as a temporary arrangement – until certain, ah, complexities are ironed out in my home city. Di Tassato will do, I consider myself of that city, or strictly of Mestra, the eastern city, but that is a nuance that need not concern you. And with whom do I have the honour of conversing?'

'Guardian Brother Thaddeus. Of the White City, Bastion, in Highguard.'

'Is it not usual to append a chapter name?' asked Rodrigo, messily biting into a ripe plum.

'Is it not usual for a Leaguer to append a House name?' queried Thaddeus. 'He opened his habit to reveal the sigil on the front of his surcoat. This is my chapter – it is a new one.'

Rodrigo gave a short barking laugh. 'Whatever! It is so difficult to keep abreast of Highborn chapters, especially the minor ones – even if one was inclined to do so.' He began to slowly lick juice from the bloomed purple skin of the plum.

'Your Excellency, you were expecting my visit – I am certain you were alerted as soon as I started asking where you might be found. You know who I am, and the chapter I represent, because you will have made it your business to know before I ever entered your chambers. I have been under your hand since I walked through the gate of the city, have I not?'

'Have you come to kill me, Highborn?'

'Do you think I should?'

Rodrigo laughed again. 'Suddenly, a dull evening has become unexpectedly rewarding!' He clapped his hands and servants rushed forward, helping Thaddeus remove his habit, and pouring scented water over his hands from a golden ewer into a golden bowl. Thaddeus carefully washed his hands, passed them over his face and hair, and then dried them on a crisp linen hand towel.

'Sit, my friend,' said Rodrigo. 'Take some food – only simple crumbs for a weekday supper, little more than peasant fare, but help yourself!' He stretched for a suckling pig on a platter, fell short, and had to rely on a servant to slide it along the packed table. Thaddeus was offered a tall chair of intricately worked black oak, seated himself, and selected a few items from the mass of dishes and bowls and arranged them on his plate.

Rodrigo took a knife and cut off one of the suckling pig's ears, then reclined back on his cushioned throne, chewing the ear, and watching Thaddeus carefully. 'I have been aware of you, Highborn,' he said. 'I know a certain amount about you, as you suggest. What I do not know is why you are seeking me, and that concerns me.'

'It need not,' said Thaddeus. 'I merely want to discuss some business with you.'

Rodrigo fanned himself with a napkin. 'I fear you may have been misdirected, I am nothing more than a simple priest, a poor pastor, struggling to tend my congregation, to keep their feet on the Sevenfold Path.' He grinned at Thaddeus. He really was quite a showman.

'Then I must have been misinformed,' said Thaddeus, holding Rodrigo's eyes. 'Perhaps there is another bishop of the same name? I was looking for a skilled and ruthless investor, who has cultivated…contacts…across the length and breadth of the Empire and elevated himself to a position of some influence and wealth from relatively inauspicious origins. A man, however, who has attracted some controversy for his willingness to embrace somewhat unorthodox means to achieve his goals.'

'And were you to find such a man, what would you ask him Highborn?'

'To consider a proposition.'

'I see. And this proposition, is it yours, or your chapter's?'

'It is on behalf of my chapter.'

Rodrigo considered for a moment. 'I feel I must warn you Thaddeus – may I call you Thaddeus? That I am a graduate from the School of Epistemology in my native city. That means I place particular care in the way I use words, and the way others use words. You, my friend, are picking your words carefully.'

'Yes.'

'Then, in one sentence, tell me what it is you want of me.'

Thaddeus considered for a moment, then said, 'To borrow a significant sum of money in order to complete building work on the new chapterhouse and finance my Exarch's campaign to become the next incumbent on the Throne Imperial.'

Rodrigo's glistening face remained impassive, although he stopped chewing on the ear. 'Taking the second item first, why should I support a Highborn candidate to replace our beloved and sadly missed Empress Lisabetta, who, as we both well know, hailed from this very city?'

'Because, as you will be fully aware, my Exarch is betrothed to a Leaguer, better yet a member of the late Empress's household. The nations of the Empire are most unlikely to follow a League Throne with another Leaguer, but in the absence of a League Throne, a League consort is a very good alternative. As a loyal citizen of the League, you could be comfortable, indeed proud, supporting a candidacy that aligns so well with your nation's interests.'

Rodrigo was watching Thaddeus closely. He did not nod or allow his expression so much as a flicker to betray what he was thinking.

Thaddeus continued, 'At a purely practical level, I can assure you the new Emperor would be most grateful to the loyal friends who supported him when he was an unknown candidate and something of an outsider. He would feel certain sympathy for those who were perhaps unfairly marginalised by the Imperial establishment in the past.'

'You are very candid.'

'Some call us blunt.'

'And why should I be remotely interested in building your chapterhouse?'

'Completion of the chapterhouse will enable us to entertain more pilgrims. The Exarch is establishing a reputation for leadership in religious and moral matters and attracting something of a following. The more pilgrims and scholars we entertain, the greater the Exarch's influence, and the greater the revenues flowing into the chapter.'

'Your Exarch is not, as far as I know, a priest. He is a mage, is he not?'

'He *is* a Highborn.'

'You appreciate how very arrogant that sounds! But I understand what you mean. The whole country is practically a seminary.'

'I'm sorry, I did not mean to be arrogant. He is a magister, a mage-priest, and has a congregation, so he does teach religion, in a formal sense.'

'I can scarcely wait to debate points of doctrine with him. And if his bid for the Throne should fail?'

'He will have established himself as a player, a candidate, a political and moral force in the Empire. Something fresh, new, energetic, someone with a clear vision. A leader-in-waiting. He has youth on his side, he will continue to build his following. There will be another opportunity – who knows what might befall an Emperor or Empress struggling to fill Lisabetta's shoes in these challenging times?'

'Indeed. And does your Exarch know you are here?'

Thaddeus's hand hesitated for a moment as he plucked a grape.

Rodrigo saw the hesitation. 'Ah, he does not. Now that is interesting. I see. I wonder what I should make of that?' Rodrigo reflected for a moment. 'Such a young man, he *is* sharp though, isn't he, your Exarch?'

'People underestimate him at their peril, he is slight, but a considerable intellect, with a fierce commitment to the Way.'

'The perfect dinner party guest,' said Rodrigo, stifling a yawn. 'I think that is enough for one night – I don't want to ruin our digestion by poring over boring business. Now, my friend, you are far from home, and I want you to make the most of our League culture. I can only imagine how brutal and plain life must be in Highguard – I have never been able to steel myself enough to visit. I have arranged appropriate lodgings for you in adjacent chambers, and had your possessions moved from the rather inappropriate lodging house you are currently occupying…'

'That really wasn't necessary.'

'My dear friend, I absolutely insist. Furthermore, you will be aware perhaps of our tradition of cicisbeo? I feel you should have some company tonight. Please allow me to introduce Cassandra, and her brother Helenus. I had no idea of your preference, so I thought it would be easier to choose between twins.'

Rodrigo indicated the furthest dark reach of his chamber, beyond the end of his long table, and Thaddeus's blood ran cold as he realised there were two more people in the room. He had accounted for Rodrigo and his three servants, but, he realised, there had been two more listening-in on their conversation, sophisticated Leaguish courtesans, skilled at lifting secrets. He wondered why his usually sharp instincts hadn't warned him. Now that Rodrigo had pointed them out, he saw them, two elegant figures wearing doll-like white full-face masks, that seemed almost to blur into the crowded opulence of Rodrigo's chamber. League masks and mirrors were hearth magic, like the Highborn's hood, veil, and bell, and that might partly explain why the twin cicisbeos had escaped Thaddeus's notice. They removed their masks without changing their relaxed lounging postures and smiled at Thaddeus. Their similarity was remarkable.

Thaddeus pushed back his heavy chair, stood, gravely bowed to the twins, and said, 'Guardian Thaddeus at your service' then remained standing. This seemed to discomfit the twins, who looked at each other, then stood, walked forward into the light, and gave elegant bows. Helenus was superbly dressed as a League bravo, thrustingly masculine with a sharply tailored velvet doublet, velvet codpiece, wine red hose and tall boots, he carried a jewelled dagger at his side. Cassandra was dressed to match, but instead of a doublet she wore a very short dress, looking both feminine and provocative, her hose and boots matched her brother's, and she carried an identical dagger.

The twins introduced themselves. 'Helenus van Holberg.'

'Cassandra van Holberg.'

'Cassandra, Helenus, I am honoured,' said Thaddeus and bowed to each of them. Once again, his reaction unsettled the twins.

Rodrigo was watching the interplay between Thaddeus and the twins wolfishly. He clapped his hands. 'Enough.' He laughed. 'I feel benevolent, and I enjoy your company Guardian Thaddeus – something I never thought I would hear myself say of a Highborn! Take them both!' Then he chuckled and added, 'A night with them *both* usually attracts a special premium!'

Thaddeus bowed low to Rodrigo. 'Your Excellency is most generous; I am quite overwhelmed. I feel myself sinking deeper in your debt.'

'I'm sure we will be able to work something out,' said Rodrigo happily.

Thaddeus remained standing. 'There has been what our Dawnish friends would call a Test of Mettle, and we each passed.' Thaddeus thought for a moment. 'No, perhaps that is a poor analogy. An *assaying*. The metal is indeed as described, business can proceed.'

Rodrigo was listening carefully as he licked morsels of food from his chubby ring-weighted fingers. 'You are very confident, Highborn.'

Thaddeus shrugged. 'I will know soon enough if I'm wrong, won't I?'

Rodrigo stopped, regarded Thaddeus for a moment, then gave one of his barking laughs. 'I could place our business in the hands of one of my ah...subordinates. It could all be concluded quite speedily, but instead I will handle it myself, and there will be a series of meetings. This is, of course, because I am rather relishing our interaction.'

Thaddeus inclined his head in a nod of acceptance. 'Thank you then for your time and your candour. If you are finding this useful and instructive, then I am gratified. That can be offset as my contribution in payment of some of the lesser debts I have already incurred.'

Rodrigo's eyes bulged, he gasped. 'My dear Guardian Thaddeus, I do believe you are made of steel.'

A small smile flickered on Thaddeus's lips. 'No, just flesh and blood.'

The bishop's vast form melted into his cushioned chair and he looked from Thaddeus to the cicisbeos and back again. He was back on safe ground. He leered at Thaddeus. 'Quite so my friend – and the night is young. As you see, I am grown old, and frail. I must content myself with these trifles.' He waved his plump hand at the groaning table, which did indeed contain trifles, along with every manner of other dessert and delicacy.

The bishop closed his eyes in contemplation, then fixed them on Thaddeus. 'Do have fun. Take advantage, abuse my hospitality, run amok, debase yourselves, be *wicked*!' Rodrigo sighed and shuddered as a thrill passed through his bulging form. 'I will just have to *imagine* what you naughty young things are getting up to.' The bishop simpered. 'Shock me Thaddeus.' He reached into a gold basin of ice and lifted an oyster to his lips, slurping the flesh from the shell. 'Shock me. I insist!'

Thaddeus made to leave, and one of Rodrigo's servants raced to move his chair and help him into his habit. The Highborn's plate held the leafed top of a small sprig of celery, an empty vine from a small cluster of grapes and three olive stones. He bowed from the waist. 'Thank you for your hospitality, Excellency. I look forward to our next meeting.'

The servant held the door, the twins glided through. Thaddeus raised his hood and followed them out. The twins tripped lightly down the stone steps that led to Roderigo's door and draped themselves around the courtyard with studied nonchalance.

Thaddeus followed more slowly, the bell at his waist giving a small chime as he took each step. He crossed to the fountain that brought water to the residents of the houses that enclosed the courtyard and took the bell from his belt. He rang it, a clean, tinkling ring, then replaced it and carefully washed his hands, then his face, then sprinkled water over his head.

'So, favoured guest,' said Cassandra, 'where do you want us?'

'And *what* is it you want?' added Helenus archly.

The two closed with Thaddeus, crossing the courtyard like smoke, insinuating themselves into his space, in his face, their three bodies touching. Helenus kissed his sister and they stared at Thaddeus, challenging him, daring him.

'Well, there is...something,' said Thaddeus diffidently.

The twins exchanged glances – *here it comes*.

'I was wondering if you might show me the sights.'

'The sights?' said Cassandra, blankly.

'Yes. You know, what it is that makes Holberg. What defines the place?'

'Why don't you just hire a palanquin?' The Leaguer, the famed cicisbeo, couldn't decide whether to be outrageously offended or utterly contemptuous, and settled on both.

Helenus yawned and peered through an open window, reached in, and stole an apple. He bit into it, regarding Thaddeus with that special look every townsman reserves for country bumpkins.

Thaddeus shrugged. 'I could, but I figure you two can get to the places everyone knows through the little alleys and byways *nobody* knows.'

The twins regarded him with increased interest. Cassandra took hold of Thaddeus's purse. 'Places like that are where a visitor from out of town can end up losing his coin – and a lot more.'

'I'm sure. Certain, in fact. So, there is no better opportunity than when my evening is the gift – no, perhaps the *property* – of Rodrigo, and I am accompanied by you two. I fancy you can look after yourselves.'

'And just what byways do you want to visit?' asked Cassandra.

'Well, it's important to see the key places that define a place, but to understand somewhere, you need to approach through the unfashionable bit, the part that the locals use. If we had time, I would get a haircut.'

'A haircut?'

'There is no better way of feeling the rhythms of a place.'

Helenus was suspicious. He stared at Thaddeus. 'Are you a spy?'

'That is a difficult question to answer convincingly.'

'Without hot irons…'

'True. But no, I am not. I live in a town, the White City, so I know how towns work. You must visit, in fact, I really insist.'

Helenus shrugged and threw the apple into the pool of the fountain. 'Well, you're the client. If that's what you want, that is what you shall have.'

As he was speaking, Cassandra backed up to Thaddeus and raised his booted foot, as one would an ox's hoof. 'The hooded cloak is good. Five-buckle fighting boots, the soles are thin enough to give you feel. They will do. The bell is hopeless.'

'I shall remove the clapper. Am I to assume I may wake up tomorrow bootless?'

Helenus ran a finger down Thaddeus's cheek. 'Darling, no Leaguer would wear those to hang on a gibbet. I *promise* you can keep them!'

Thaddeus freed himself from Cassandra and regarded the twins for a moment. 'I was wondering, I know you are working, but I wondered if you might want to change first.'

Cassandra put her mouth against his ear and tickled his earlobe with the tip of her tongue. 'You want to watch us dressing?'

'No, not especially, but I am curious to know how you look when you are yourselves. I'm guessing rather swaggery bravos? I am also very interested to know if you always dress as each other.'

He looked up at Rodrigo's doorway at the top of the flight of steps. 'Do you always do it? Was the Bishop in on it – was it one of his little games? Or is it that when you are in thrall to a man like that you take any and every opportunity you can to score your own small points?'

The twins were frozen, staring at him wide-eyed. The real Cassandra raised her hand and started an incantation. Thaddeus took her hand and stilled her. 'I am not using magic I am using my head.'

'When did you know?'

'As soon as you moved. You both move like cats, but differently.'

'Are all Highborn like you?'

'Are all Leaguers like you?'

Thaddeus looked up at the patch of sky framed by the roofs of the buildings surrounding the courtyard. 'It's dark, the moon will be rising, and we are on the bishop's time. You have a town to show me – unless, of course, you're

89

embarrassed about it, compared to a place like the White City.' He looked with feigned concern at the twins. 'You know I'll completely understand if you are…'

Both twins threw their heads back and laughed aloud, a flash of even white teeth. They sprang, every move a dance step started with a skip. They didn't so much run as flow, like quicksilver, fleeting shadows, and Thaddeus, lithe and no slouch on his own terms, thumped along behind.

Upstairs, at a tall lancet window, Rodrigo stood and watched the three depart the courtyard. He let the velvet drape fall and took a draught from a jewelled cup. He savoured the wine, putting his head back, pursing his lips and noisily sucking in air to release the bouquet. He swallowed the mouth-warmed wine with a wet gulp, gave a satisfied belch, and returned to the laden table.

VII

Gwin was hungry. She was also curled up under her faux-fur blanket feeling a little underdressed. The sun had gone in, and it was cooler now. She pondered slipping on just her black kurta and churidars base kit. She decided she really liked the below-the-knee length silky shirt, with its standing collar, and the trousers that were baggy at the top and then hugged her calves and fitted brilliantly under her five-buckle larp boots, or her new armour. She could put on Thaddeus's travelling habit and dodge out to the out-of-character food stalls for a noodle lunch, the trouble was, that way she would be missing an opportunity to see the game in full swing, mid-way through play. So that meant getting back into kit again. Goodness, this was so *demanding*. She groaned and rummaged for the tape. At least, she would be wearing Thaddeus's soft kit, no gambeson, hauberk, vambraces or greaves. She sniffed the kurta; the thin fabric had dried out and she probably wouldn't smell much worse than anyone else. Note-to-self: buy another kurta and churidars for next time. At least they were cheap and didn't take up any space at all. She realised she would need something between the kurta and the habit, and that meant the surcoat of course, which was splashed with blood. Nothing else for it. Goodness, she was learning lessons you just couldn't get posing in front of the bedroom mirror excitedly trying on your latest mail order costume delivery.

Gwin-as-Thaddeus was picking her way through the Highguard tents, headed towards the centre of Anvil, when a hand crashed down on her shoulder and she jumped.

'I'm still very worried about your sword!'

Gwin looked around, and saw the cataphract, in soft kit, with a bloodied bandage on her neck and her right arm in a sling. She grinned. 'Hello Sister! I am delighted to see you on your feet.'

'Largely, thanks to you.'

'I think there's an extremely brave mage we both owe a drink to.'

'That is true. Adjutant Taliah,' said the cataphract, holding out her good arm.

Gwin gripped it. 'Guardian Brother Thaddeus.'

'Hello Thaddeus, I don't think I've seen you around.'

'I'm new to Anvil,' said Gwin-as-Thaddeus, giving the code phrase that meant "I'm a brand-new player".

Taliah's eyes widened. 'Really? You seemed very…assured on the battlefield.'

'Once you picked me up of the floor!'

'It had its moments. Where are you off to?'

'Exploring – and finding some food. You?'

'The Military Council.'

'May I walk with you?'

'Of course!'

Gwin was learning to learn. As they walked, she prompted Taliah to explain how the Military Council worked. Adjutant Taliah wasn't actually on the council but carried messages and stood-in for people at meetings, and desperately wanted to be a general and take her place at the planning table. Gwin began to understand, there was *getting* a hat, and there was *keeping* a hat – with a queue of ambitious players lining up to take your place as soon as you dropped your guard.

Gwin-as-Thaddeus bid farewell to Taliah and a couple of friendly generals, and, at their suggestion, popped her head in at the Senate, and crossed over to the Hub, where she spent a while reading the amazing selection of in-character posters and notices. Now Gwin was seriously hungry and retraced her steps to a big in-character eatery, bought cheesy chips and a Coke Zero with her phone, and asked if she could squeeze on to the end of a table full of Varushkans, which was odd, because she never would have done that before.

All the nations had a distinctive look-and-feel, so you could recognise immediately where a character came from. Likewise, name conventions, so you could tell by a name on a list that the character was Highborn, or a Leaguer, or from the Brass Coast or wherever. The Varushkans had a Slavic style, drawing on the medieval Rus for inspiration, with a heavy dollop of Brothers Grimm dark fairytale added for good measure. Somewhere along the way, they had started adopting a Russian accent, which was hilarious and totally brilliant, especially as the players carried it off so well. Gwin gave the 'I'm new to Anvil' code phrase, and the Varushkans were charming, falling over themselves to tell her about their homeland, where doors and windows were barred and shuttered at dusk, and the shadowed woods of night were filled with unblinking eyes. Never, they told her, *never* stray from the path! She finished her cheesy chips with invitations to all sorts of sinister-sounding Varushkan places, governed by Boyars and surrounded by fell and haunted forests, she absolutely couldn't wait.

Gwin was slightly vexed about the sword business, and so Gwin-as-Thaddeus spent a good while visiting the various weapon stalls, weighing up options. Gwin discovered she knew that the way a sword behaves in the hand was 'heft' and wondered if that was overspill from Thaddeus or something she'd picked up from one of the sword masters or fight arrangers at work. She also discovered she could do a sort of spinning thing with the sword, which she definitely hadn't been able to do previously. She might be Gwin-as-Thaddeus, rather than Thaddeus-as-Thaddeus, but her character was becoming a bit of a force to be reckoned with.

Suddenly the armourer was standing beside her. 'Try this one,' he said, taking a smart cross-hilt off the rack. 'These are weighted, they feel just like a real sword.'

'So far, that hasn't really proven to be a problem,' said Gwin, sniffily. 'The armour has been great, by the way.'

'I'm glad.'

'I went looking for you, but the tent was gone.'

'It wasn't necessary.'

'Practically or narratively?'

He laughed. 'You're getting the hang of this.'

Gwin swung the sword a few times. Like Thaddeus, she was happier with the short-bladed one. 'I was worried Thaddeus was riding around in my head, just like I am in his.'

'And was he?'

'You mean you don't know?'

'What you lot get up to constantly surprises me.'

'How can that be?'

'Edward Elgar said, "There is music in the air, music all around us; the world is full of it, and you simply take as much as you require". It's the same with stories, Gwin. Sometimes I can't write fast enough, you and your friends go faster than I can keep up.'

'Didn't someone say that every block of stone has a statue inside it, and it's the job of the sculptor to find it?'

'Michelangelo. Not the turtle, the other one.'

'I'm not sure about this sword.' She looked around, but he had melted into the crowd. Gwin shook her head, she put the sword back on the rack and wondered where to go next. A tour of the nations was definitely in order. Having spent most of her time in-character slaughtering orcs, she felt obliged to go and visit the Imperial Orcs. They were 'friendlies' – the descendants of orc slaves freed long ago, who had continued to live in the Empire, mostly to fight as Imperial legionaries, and eventually been rewarded with a province of their own. They were fiercely loyal to the Empire, and there was no love lost between them and the barbarian orcs. That said, to many Imperial citizens, and especially Highborn, they were still just orcs.

'Yes?' said the orc.

'I'm exploring, I'm new to Anvil.'

The orc leant across, his arm blocking her way. 'Have you come to enslave us, Highborn?'

Gwin remembered a conversation she had with Beth about the Imperial Orcs. Their basic kit was much more elaborate than the other nations, and when they were in character, they had to wear latex prosthetic masks, which was not only hot and uncomfortable, but meant that there were no facial expressions, so they had to use their voices and body language. As a result, they tended to be really accomplished players. The orcs were supposed to be rather feral and chaotic, but they were actually serious achievers in the game. There was even an Imperial Orc cardinal, which was pretty good going for a species without a soul. They were not human, they could not breed with humans and did not become lineaged – and 'new to Anvil' or not, they were going to make sure she played her heart out.

She hesitated, and suddenly Gwin-as-Thaddeus looked straight at the orc and said, 'You're too old to be house trained. But if you've got a litter, I might be interested in some of the stronger ones.'

The orc stared at her, and Gwin wondered where on earth that had come from, and whether she was about to be beaten senseless, then the orc roared with laughter and speeded her on her way into their camp with a thump on the back that made the Dawnish battle captain's slap feel like a lover's caress. She thought she might have lost a filling.

Gwin liked the orc camp immediately. It looked great; elaborately dressed, with stumps and skulls and lamps and a lot of rope. There was a pit fight in progress, between a bare-chested Marcher and a big orc; it involved a lot a grunting and shouting and a certain amount of blood. A noisy throng of orcs and Marchers were cheering on their respective champions.

Gwin-as-Thaddeus stood watching the fight for a while. A particularly grubby orc came to stand beside her. He was drinking beer out of a tankard shaped from a length of horn and seemed to have scant interest in the outcome of the pit fight. Gwin had been fighting real orcs, but it was amazing how intimidating the player-character orcs were. Okay, so it was a rubber over-the-head prosthetic, cut away around the eyes and mouth, and the exposed skin painted with Snazz face paint, but they were still totally intimidating, and their ragged, multi-layered outfits were incredible.

'Your turn next Highborn,' said the orc.

'That's quite alright, I think I'll just watch today.'

'Scared of getting beaten?'

Gwin shook her head. 'No, it's just that I've already got orc blood all over my surcoat.' She felt she was living dangerously, but her inner Thaddeus was clearly determined to make an impression. 'Guardian Thaddeus,' said Gwin-as-Thaddeus, offering an arm.

The orc gripped her arm. 'Redhand Feresh,' said the orc. He pointed to a scrap of leather on his war skirt that had the three bold strokes of the feresh rune crudely painted on it, and another with a red hand. 'I can read runes,' he said proudly. 'I'm a shaman, do you want me to read your future?'

Gwin-as-Thaddeus thought about it for a moment. 'Tempting, but no, I think that might spoil the suspense, but I'll take a drink if you're offering.'

The orc steered her towards a rustic bench by a tree stump. 'Do you want beer?' he waved his tankard. 'Or something without alcohol?'

'What are you having?'

Feresh put down his tankard and opened his grimy robe, furtively showing Gwin a bottle in a leather carrier hanging from his belt. He pulled out the bottle, it had a parchment label.

Basilisk Venom? queried Gwin.

'I get it from a Highborn.'

'Do you indeed? And does he also sell you beads and mirrors and crates of rusty crossbows?'

The orc looked puzzled.

'Does it come in pints?' asked Gwin, feeling that a LOTR reference was long overdue.

The orc fished in a pouch on his war skirt and produced two shot glasses and put them on the tree stump. Gwin was impressed and tempted to ask if he could also produce a bowl of pork scratchings and some pimento stuffed olives but thought that might be tempting fate.

Feresh poured Basilisk Venom into each of the shot glasses until they overflowed. Gwin-as-Thaddeus watched impassively. Gwin really knew how to play this game – she had once spent six weeks filming in Moscow. She dimly remembered a bizarre day eating slices of kiwi fruit and drinking lighter-fuel grade vodka out of a paper cup. The Russians were mystified by the Anglo-American concept of a dry film unit, as indeed were the French and Italians she had worked with, which probably explained why the Hollywood–Pinewood axis made more blockbusters, but everyone else had more fun. She had also spent some time – five minutes or five months, depending on whether or not you were running on an *Inception* timescale – living in a battlefront officers' mess, drinking whisky and soda with the other officers, and service rum with her sergeant. The later was supposed to be watered-down, but Sergeant Jones viewed the instruction as a serving suggestion and chose to disregard it entirely.

Gwin-as-Thaddeus picked up the shot glass, it was worrying that the drink was exactly the same colour as the liquid flush in the portaloos. With an open throat, she downed it in one. Then put the empty glass upside down on the tree stump. There was no smacking of lips, or rolling of eyes, or any other histrionics. Gwin just downed it and sat impassively, which was not at all what Feresh was expecting. Behind Gwin's imperturbable façade, damage-control parties were making an urgent assessment. They reported back that the booze had made a soft landing in a large portion of cheesy chips, and that all systems were still nominal and functioning. Feresh was nonplussed, he took his glass and downed it, forgetting that the upper lip of his mask was over his real upper lip, got slightly tangled, and the last few drops of Basilisk Venom went down the wrong way, resulting in an explosion of coughing. Gwin-as-Thaddeus didn't rush around to slap him on the back, but just watched until he had just about regained his composure. 'One more, and then I really must be off.'

Feresh shakily poured another shot, and Gwin-as-Thaddeus banged it down. This time amber lights started to appear on control panels, and the chief engineer reported that the shot struck close to the waterline. Another one like that and he couldn't guarantee steering or propulsion, and sensors were down to sixty percent.

'Have another,' said Feresh.

'No, thank you. I don't want to wake up turning on a spit over your fire.'

Feresh downed his shot and laughed, dabbing his streaming eyes with the sleeve of his robe. Gwin-as-Thaddeus stood, saluted with a clenched fist to the chest and a bowed head. Feresh had never been saluted by a Highborn and was surprised and flattered. Gwin carefully made her way out of the orc camp and back towards the centre of Anvil.

Gwin was happy and feeling a warm glow. She couldn't believe she had been so nervy and unconfident before. This role-play thing was easy, she might even go somewhere where there was a crowd and make a speech or do some stand-up. She pondered joining another skirmish but reflected that would require putting on armour and killing orcs, neither of which she was in the mood for. A grown-up voice in her head was telling her to go easy, because there was quite a lot of Basilisk Venom in her system, and she had no idea what that actually was, beyond the fact it looked and smelt rather like windscreen de-icer – which, had she still been in Russia, would have been exactly what it was. It was possible, the grown-up voice reminded her, that she might not be *entirely* in control. She realised she should have visited the Navarr camp, which was in the woods next door to the orcs, but it was too late. She knew, too, she was avoiding Dawn, partly because the Dawnish were determined to engage with her, and she was a bit shy, and mostly because her name was Guinevere, and, in a way, she had been Dawnish all her life.

Coward, she thought and headed for Dawn. When she got there, she found it heavily decorated with flowers, especially roses, banners fluttering, and really rather pretty and Victorian Arthurian-fantasy-like – apart from a brutal battle that was taking place in the tournament square between an armoured Dawnish and a ferocious female Imperial Orc, who was sitting on the Dawnish warrior's breastplate, hitting him on the head as he lay in the grass dizzy from being shoulder-charged. The referee hadn't called it yet, but there could only be one winner. Gwin-as-Thaddeus declined the opportunity to take part in the tourney, toured the camp, and chatted to a few Dawnish, determining that the battle captain and his buddies were back at the Sentinel Gate, skirmishing again. Job done, time to move on. It was incredible how teemingly busy Anvil was, with thousands of people dashing about in character:

meetings, rituals, fights, deals, assignations, intrigues, love affairs – births, deaths, and marriages. There were even occasional visitors from the magical realms, elaborately made-up Heralds bringing great chunks of game plot to a lucky few.

'Welcome to the Brass Coast! A Highborn without a rosary? That just won't do!' The flamboyant Freeborn bead-seller laughed. She had a pile of necklaces around her neck, rosaries up one arm, and bracelets up the other. There was a selection of rosaries with different colours and styles of beads. Several of them were made with tiny skulls, and it was clear that the seller's business model in the rosary sector was targeted at Highguard. Gwin-as-Thaddeus ignored the skulls and picked out a simple row of amber coloured beads.

'Only a crown,' said the bead-seller hopefully.

Gwin-as-Thaddeus explained that she only had twelve rings on her, and the bead-seller looked disappointed. Then in a flash of inspiration, Gwin added, 'Unless you'd take an ingot of green iron.' The seller's eyes lit up, and Gwin handed over all her coins and one of the little ingots and got a seven-bead amber-coloured rosary in return, with a Labyrinth medallion on the end of it. As Gwin walked away she started to wonder what the exchange rate actually was for green iron, and how she might find out, and it suddenly occurred to her that this might be what people meant by "the trading game".

The chapter camp felt like an oasis of calm when Gwin finally got back. She snuck into her tent before anyone could notice her, took off Thaddeus's habit and surcoat, made herself comfortable on her camp bed and picked up her rosary. She simply could not be a Highborn unless she could recite her catechism, the Seven Virtues. The idea of the Virtues was borrowed, Gwyn knew, from Roman society, and the Seven Virtues had been deliberately chosen to stimulate play, making players do things that drove the game forward, and drove them forward in the game. They were different to traditional European society, and deliberately so: if the Virtues had been poverty, chastity, and obedience, it would have been rather a quiet weekend.

On top of the chapterhouse tower, the Exarch and Thaddeus had named them in alphabetical order. Gwin struggled to remember, Ambition, Pride, Wisdom, Vigilance, Courage, wealth…no…Prosperity. What the hell was the other one? Loyalty – of course, only Thaddeus's dedication! She tried again, Ambition, Courage, Loyalty, Pride, Prosperity, Vigilance…er…Wisdom. And again, *spare the rod and spoil the child.* She flicked the beads on her rosary, Ambition, Courage, Loyalty, Pride, Prosperity, Vigilance, Wisdom. And again, *show clean hands*, Ambition, Courage, Loyalty, Pride, Prosperity, Vigilance, Wisdom. And again, Ambition, Courage, Loyalty, Pride, Prosperity, Vigilance, Wisdom. And again: Ambition, Courage, Loyalty…

VIII

'Aren't we leaving the city?' panted Thaddeus, as the three ran through the dark streets. He recognised the great gateway, its pointed-roofed towers and barbicans. They stopped on the innermost drawbridge and stood together in the moonlight, looking down into the dry moat, watched by a bored guard with a decorated partisan polearm over his shoulder. The twins closed up to Thaddeus and held him tightly between them. There was a caress, a kiss, and another, tentative, then passionate. The guard watched, coughed uncomfortably, and embarrassed, turned and retreated under the arch of the gate to give them a little privacy. As soon as his back was turned, the twins swung onto the huge chains of the drawbridge, climbing the links like a ladder. Thaddeus, still slightly dizzy from being unexpectedly kissed, realised why his boot soles had been a subject for inspection, and climbed quickly up after the twins before the guard turned around and patrolled back again.

On either side of the drawbridge, the massive chains hung from huge timbers, oak beams that extended back into the gatehouse and could swing up into slots in the face of the gatehouse when the drawbridge was raised. Cassandra sprinted along the beam and wriggled through the slot into the gatehouse. Helenus was close behind her. A pigeon clattered away from the gatehouse as Thaddeus gingerly stood on the beam, not daring to look down at the rock-floored moat far below. He could see the guard's shadow moving on the roadway as he walked back to his post, and Thaddeus dashed, reached the slot, and somehow squeezed through into an empty and dusty guard chamber. There were no furnishings, just a carpet of pigeon droppings, a raised portcullis and its windlass, and on either side of the room the great counterbalance weights of the drawbridge. The twins put their fingers to their lips, then, moving silently as ghosts, slipped through a small doorway in the corner of the room and started up a stone stair that spiralled up to the battlements.

They stood together, high up on the flat lead roof of the gatehouse. Between the great loopholed battlements the moonlit view out over the mountain pass that provided the only access to the city was stunning. Three flagpoles, cut from the tallest pine trees, thrust high above their heads, carrying the embroidered banners of Holberg, the League, and Empire. The huge flags hung limp, barely stirring in the still night air. Crossing to the back of the gatehouse, Thaddeus took in the gablet rooftops and hipped gables of Holberg itself, so different from the profile of his own White City. 'Couldn't we have tipped the guard a crown and used the door?' He asked in a whisper.

The twins pondered for a moment. '*Possibly*', said Cassandra.

'But where's the fun in that?' asked Helenus.

Thaddeus shook his head, his shoulders heaving with silent laughter.

They stood and took in the views, it was one of those nights when the moon shone with a burnished intensity, a bright silver light. They looked down on the rooftops. Helenus leaned against the battlement. 'In the city, everyone lives on top of each other, everyone knows each other's business, everyone has an opinion.' He said quietly, 'I'm sure your city is no different Thaddeus. For us it's worse, because we belong to everyone. Sometimes you need to be invisible, just to keep your sanity. That is why Leaguers make a big thing of masks, you have to keep something for yourself. Long ago we learned to survive here by finding our own secret ways around the city – so it was strange to hear you talking about the hidden by-ways nobody knows.'

'My city is not so different,' said Thaddeus. 'That's why I spend most of my time away.'

There were steps down to the wall walk, battlements on one side, and a long drop to the street on the other. Cassandra was walking backwards, in front of Thaddeus. 'Of course, the city is famous for its fortifications – we have a dozen walls,' she said proudly.

He grabbed her arm, terrified in case she stumbled and fell off the wall. 'How long was the city besieged?' he asked.

'It held out against the Druj for thirty years,' said Helenus.

The innermost wall was tall enough at the point they were walking to overlook the others, and so was immensely high. On the city side, they looked across a sea of pantile roofs and crow-stepped gables topped with narrow brick chimneys. There was soft yellow lamplight behind the shuttered windows, and the streets were lost in deep shadow far below. At some points, the buildings touched the wall, and the three sightseers stepped off the walk onto a roof, scrambled up one side and down the other, and then climbed an even bigger one. The highest point of the roof was flat, and they walked along, looking down over the city.

'The Guilds,' said Cassandra, pointing to the rooftops of several great buildings. Thaddeus looked, then looked again, confirming that the nearest gargoyle really did have an expression of stony innocence and a mouthful of pigeon feathers.

'And you get a really good view of the Grand Clocktower,' said Helenus, which they did, marvelling at the clock's painted and gilded dials and pointers.

You have a very big clock, murmured Thaddeus.

'What?' said Helenus.

'I'm sorry – something just suddenly popped into my head,' said Thaddeus, embarrassed. Gwin's consciousness, remembering another time and place, would have blushed if it could.

'The university is also an important feature of the city,' said Cassandra.

'Where is that?' asked Thaddeus, straining to look.

'You're standing on it.'

'I think we should get some food,' said Helenus.

'Where's the best place to eat?' asked Thaddeus.

The twins thought about it. 'Probably an inn near your old lodgings,' said Helenus. 'Let's go!'

They were observing the inn from across the street. There was a throng of fashionable Leaguers outside the door, the place was busy and even turning people away. 'Unless you brought quite a lot of money with you, you probably can't afford to eat there, but from here we can sneak into the kitchen without being spotted,' said Cassandra quietly. Thaddeus nodded, reached into a pocket inside his habit, pulled out a square of folded fabric and shook it out to reveal a black veil. He lifted off his iron circlet and handed it to Helenus, then put the veil over his head, replaced the circlet and put his hood up. His face became less than indistinct, it was almost as if there was no head under the hood of his habit.

'What are you doing?' asked Cassandra.

'That is quite worrying,' said Helenus.

'Says the people with the white masks!' Thaddeus took the twins' arms and before they could protest, strode across the street, through the crowd and in at the front entrance of the tavern.

The proprietor looked up from a table full of customers, saw the three of them and rushed over. 'I'm sorry we are late,' said Thaddeus, 'Is the room ready?'

'Room?' asked the host, staring into the fathomless darkness of Thaddeus's hood.

'Bishop Rodrigo said his servants had booked us a private room.'

'Bishop Rodrigo?' The poor man was hypnotised by Thaddeus's faceless silhouette, and now had the dark form of Rodrigo the Iron Hand sliding into his befuddled consciousness. He recognised the twins, of course, and could see they were working. They draped themselves on the mysterious Highborn and watched the innkeeper with big wide eyes. 'Of course, of course.' He looked at the twins. 'The alcove room on the left? I'll be with you directly to take your order. I'll have a bottle of wine sent in.'

The twins nodded and led Thaddeus to a discreet room on the ground floor furnished with a table and some couches where they made themselves comfortable. The twins stared at

Thaddeus with open admiration. 'You are a *bad* Highborn!' laughed Cassandra.

'You have no idea. I told you I grew up in a city.'

'Please take that veil off,' begged Helenus, 'it feels like you're going to steal our souls.'

'There's a thought. No, not yet, let's just get some food. I had something with Rodrigo, but you two must be starving.'

'Famished!' said Cassandra.

The host bustled in with a bottle and three glasses. 'What can I get you to eat?'

'Do you have crunchy little balls?' asked Thaddeus from behind the veil.

'W-what?'

'I believe our guest means bitterballen,' said Helenus. 'That's an excellent idea, perhaps we could have a selection, a real flavour of Holberg? Can you do bamischijf? And frikandel of course – we can't let him leave the city without a taste of Holberg sausage.'

Relieved that he was not going to have to conjure up more than a table of bar snacks, the host was obsequiousness personified. 'An excellent idea! May I suggest our local beer, instead of the wine?' he asked, carefully staring above Thaddeus's hood.

'I can see why Bishop Rodrigo recommended you so highly. Thank you,' said Thaddeus graciously. And the innkeeper bowed his way out of the room.

They were back in the street but feeling comfortably full of rich, stodgy Holberg delicacies and beer. 'I can't believe you got the innkeeper to send the bill to Rodrigo!' said Cassandra, shaking her head. She had helped herself to a fistful of sugared almonds and offered one to Thaddeus, but he declined.

'Well, he did tell me to abuse his hospitality and shock him. And we *were* quite restrained, we could have ordered Lansipari crayfish or something. I think he will see the joke, and whatever happens, I suspect he'll make sure he gets his own back.' Thaddeus smiled.

'Didn't he also tell you to be wicked and debase yourself?' Teased Helenus.

'I'm here for the week, no need to rush things. That was just what was needed – really good – thank you both. What now?'

'How about the theatre?' said Cassandra. 'That's very Holberg.'

'Sounds like a good idea.'

It quickly became apparent from their unconventional approach, over two walls and via the roof of lean-to, that the twins were not intending to queue for tickets. Helenus got to work on a window with his jewelled dagger and the three slipped into the theatre. Thaddeus had never seen anything but street theatre, and then usually religious stuff or something to mark a nation's national day. It took him a while to get his bearings. He realised he was looking down on a stage, with two actors in mid-performance, lit by a row of footlights, lamps in front of mirrored reflectors. Behind the footlights Thaddeus could just make out the faces of an audience, disappearing into darkness. He could feel the charge of magic in the air, an unfamiliar sort, but there, nonetheless.

Thaddeus was as interested in the building as the play. The area above the stage was tall, its ceiling lost in darkness, so that the painted scenery could be hauled up on ropes.

Thaddeus noted the various backgrounds hanging ready to be lowered into position. After a while the twins indicated they were bored, and it was time to move on. Cassandra led the way along a precarious walkway that hung dizzyingly above the stage. It didn't quite cross the full width, and she selected one of the many ropes tied off the handrail, looked up, pulled it a few times to test, and then swung lightly across to the landing by the far wall, hooked her legs over the rail and slipped silently onto the boards. She indicated Thaddeus should go next and swung the rope back. Thaddeus caught it, looked down at the stage below, and swung. He didn't quite get his legs over the rail, and before Casandra could catch him, he swung back, not quite reaching the point where he had started. Helenus leant out but couldn't reach him either. Thaddeus was hanging, and in real danger of falling onto the stage. It was a potentially lethal predicament, but also absurdly funny. He started to swing himself, to get sufficient momentum to reach Cassandra, who was both alarmed and giggling. It was Thaddeus's legs swinging rhythmically in the heavens that caught the eye of one of the actors.

The players were in the midst of a performance of *The Steel Throne*, enjoying a successful season at one of Holberg's foremost theatres, and were not expecting to see a black-habited Highborn swinging gently in the upper reaches of the stage, invisible to the audience, but a hypnotic fascination to the thespian just about to deliver the next line. He stood open-mouthed. There was a silence that went beyond dramatic and slipped into uncomfortable. There came a '*psst*' from the prompter at the front of the stage, but the actor was fixated by the drama playing out above his head, as

Cassandra leaned out to get a fingertip grip on Thaddeus and pull him to the landing.

'*A map!*' hissed the prompter.

The actor stood transfixed.

'*A map!*' said the prompter, quite loudly. Someone in the front row of the audience sniggered.

Thaddeus didn't have the momentum, he couldn't get close enough to Cassandra, and his arms were getting tired. He made a huge effort, swung with his whole body and she grabbed his legs and he slid over the rail. She took the rope and he fell to his hands and knees, giggling helplessly with relief and the sheer ridiculousness of the situation. The actor was still frozen, watching the antics above. '*A map, a street map!*' the prompter almost shouted. The audience was starting to laugh.

Suddenly, the actor remembered where he was, remembered this was Act II, Scene IV of *The Steel Throne*, looked about, blinked, stared at the audience, and delivered his line. '*A map? A street map! You need more than a map of the streets to navigate this city, friend. There are rules to this city, break them, and the Prince will break you.*' There were cheers.

Cassandra was laughing so much she could barely stand. She threw the rope back to Helenus, who managed the swing in one. The twins lifted Thaddeus off his knees, Helenus unfastened a window, and they jumped clear of the theatre, onto the roof of a shed in the yard.

They were in the theatre's yard, surrounded by discarded scenery flats and theatrical clutter, laughing so hard they thought they might die. Cassandra had her legs crossed at the knee and ankle and seemed to be in imminent danger of an accident. Helenus was lying on the ground, clutching his sides, apparently to prevent the rupture of internal organs, and Thaddeus was just crying, barely able to breath. Slowly they got control of themselves. The perfectly applied kohl eyeliner and shadow that the twins wore was now blurred and smudged, and in that imperfection, they had Thaddeus. He sat on the ground, his back against the theatre wall, head bowed, arms rested on his knees. The agonising spasms of helpless laughter were gone, replaced with a sort of inner calm; more than anything he needed a pipe and some pipeweed. He looked at Cassandra and Helenus and felt tightness across his chest. It was real, physical, rooted in his diaphragm, but it was also so much more, and he shook his head with the helplessness of it.

What made the twins so spectacularly successful, so sought after, was not any grotesque coupling that Rodrigo's fevered imagination might concoct, it was simply that everyone who met them *needed* to fall in love with them, to slide helplessly, knowingly, and consciously under their spell. It was a path many had trodden before, and doubtless many more would follow, but for each, that moment when they looked at the twins and their heart melted within them, would be as fresh as the year's first fall of snow. Thaddeus shook his head and cursed. Another round to Rodrigo. Helenus was kneeling beside Cassandra, tying up the points holding her sleeve to her doublet, his sister scolding him for his ineptness. Watching the two of them, Thaddeus wondered if he could trust his legs to carry him. He had it, and he had it bad.

'Bakers' Street, then fish?' Suggested Cassandra.

'You think?' asked Helenus.

'Yes!' Cassandra jumped up, shrugging her brother off and leant and pulled at Thaddeus's hand.

'Come on!' she cried.

She spun, and almost flew, jumping lightly on boxes and bales to get on the top of the theatre's high boundary wall, then running full pelt along its narrow crown. The two boys exchanged glances and leapt after her.

'That's the Bakers' Street,' whispered Cassandra.

'And this is Bakers' Street Backs,' whispered Helenus.

The three of them were on the meeting point of two walls, crouched, looking down into a row of ramshackle yards. There were various privies, storehouses, sheds, and outbuildings. The twins obviously had a target in mind. Helenus sprinted silently along the wall towards a structure, light-coloured in the night. The other two followed. Helenus lowered himself from the wall, hung at the extent of his arms, then let go, dropping, to land in silence. Cassandra inclined her head to indicate Thaddeus should go next. He ran along the wall, lowered himself awkwardly, then landed with a scuff. Cassandra was already on the wall above him when he landed and winced and shook her head.

She swung lightly down, and they headed for the building. Thaddeus realised it had walls of something like muslin, stretched over a frame. It was actually a flyscreen. Helenus carefully opened the door, lifting it, taking the weight to prevent the hinges from squeaking. Inside were three big wooden bins containing the waste of a bakery. There was a smell of new bread, and old bread, and burnt bread and mould. Cassandra set to in the bins, identifying the less-spoiled loaves and passing them to Helenus. He pulled down Thaddeus's hood and started cramming in one-ring loaves and whatever else Cassandra had salvaged. Thaddeus started to protest but was silenced with a hand over his mouth.

Suddenly, there was an insistent barking from the baker's house. In an instant the twins were out of the flyscreen shed and pushing Thaddeus towards the wall. Helenus crouched with his back to the wall and made a stirrup with his hands. Thaddeus stepped quickly into the stirrup and launched himself up, throwing his arms over the wall, then swinging his legs up onto the wall and down behind, so he could reach down securely for Cassandra, who was already standing in Helenus's hands. Thaddeus lifted Cassandra on to the wall, and together they stretched down to take Helenus's wrists and lift him bodily up beside them. Throughout Thaddeus was uncomfortably aware of a cargo of spoilt bread rattling and scuffing around the back of his neck.

The bakery door swung open; a yellow rectangle lit by the flickering glow of flames heating the ovens. A big dog came hurtling out and dashed madly along the foot of the wall snarling and barking. A figure was silhouetted in the doorway, glimpsed as the three bread thieves dashed away. There was a mechanical "*thunk*", followed by a whirring sound, and a poorly aimed crossbow bolt clattered against the stonework above their heads. They crisscrossed walls, vaulted over a balcony, and then another, skidded along a polished marble hall, tumbled down some steps and were suddenly in a smart avenue a couple of blocks from the street of the bakers. They straightened up, and slowed to a dignified swagger, like any three bravos on a night out.

It was a long street, shaded from the bright moon by tall buildings on either side and lit at intervals by lamps that cast a yellow light. It was against this light that four figures appeared further up, a group of bravos walking towards them. Thaddeus and the twins were not looking for any more excitement, they crossed to the opposite side of the road and kept walking. The four figures crossed to the same side.

'Friends of yours?' asked Thaddeus quietly.

'I don't think so,' said Cassandra.

'I thought you knew everyone?'

'It's quite a big city.'

'They're not from here,' said Helenus, 'Temeschwar by the look of them.'

The four visitors from the northernmost League city were obviously looking to spice up a night out. They were wearing half-masks, calf-length boots, expensively embroidered doublets trimmed with fur, and carrying long slim dress swords with elaborate hilts. They were young, arrogant, bored, and slightly drunk – looking for trouble, and too conceited and foolish to understand they had most certainly found it. They stopped in front of Thaddeus and the twins. One of them walked up to Thaddeus. 'Greetings!' she said.

Thaddeus surveyed the four of them. 'Are you the leader?'

She grinned and hooked her fingers in her belt and looked back at the other three. 'If you like.'

'*The alpha bravo*?'

'What?' She was mystified.

'Sorry,' said Thaddeus. 'I'm getting these random thoughts popping into my head tonight.' Gwin had been rather proud of that, she didn't normally do jokes. She made a mental note not to again. Ever.

'A matched set of cicisbeo, Highborn?' said the bravo. 'We've been looking for some company, we'll take them from here,' she eyed the twins appraisingly.

Thaddeus put his arms around the twins' waists and held them close. 'No, I don't think so.'

The bravo looked at Thaddeus, then walked around them, pausing behind with surprise. 'Why is your hood full of bread?'

'I've been wondering the same thing,' said Thaddeus.

'You're quite the eccentric. Are you wealthy? You must be to afford these. Let them go with my friends, and you and I can go and spend some of your money. I'll even let you keep the bread!' She patted Helenus's bottom through his short dress. 'She's sweet, but what's she got that I haven't?'

'Do you want to tell her, or should I?' Thaddeus asked Helenus.

Cassandra looked at the bravo over Thaddeus's shoulder. 'Interesting doublets,' she said, 'so traditional. Did you make them yourselves?'

The bravo ran her finger down Cassandra's cheek. 'I think we might have some fun, you and I.'

Thaddeus felt Cassandra moving away from him. 'Don't kill them,' he said.

'We won't!' laughed the bravo. 'We'll just teach them some manners and send them on their way when we're done.'

'I wasn't talking to you.'

In a flash Cassandra's forehead connected with the bridge of the bravo's nose and there was a sound like someone stepping on an apple box. The bravo dropped in a heap as if she'd been poleaxed. The other three fumbled to draw their long slim swords. Thaddeus watched with professional interest. 'I've heard about these, but I've never seen them. Those must be the longest swords *ever* – are you trying to compensate or something?'

The second bravo lunged at Thaddeus, who stepped out of his way as he stumbled past, caught the sword and twisted it out of his hand, then, holding the blade, hit his astonished assailant very hard over the back of the head with the beautifully wrought steel hilt. He staggered two paces before falling face down on the cobbles. Cassandra easily parried the third bravo's sword with her dagger and kicked him full strength in the fork, which just left Helenus to parry the last bravo's sword on his forearm, snatch it from her hand and break it over his knee. There were three Temeschwari on the floor – two silent and one groaning quite loudly – and another on tiptoe with Helenus holding the hilt and forte of a rapier under her chin. 'Run along,' said Helenus, and she did.

'That was invigorating,' said Thaddeus, examining the sword he had taken. He weighed it in his hand, swung it a couple of times and balanced it on his finger, before tossing it into the shadows.

'You've never seen us fight,' said Cassandra, rubbing her forehead. 'How did you know we would?'

'It was an assumption, based on the fact that your idea of a walking tour of your hometown involves breaking into a fortress, scaling the most famous walls in the Empire, jumping over rooftops, stealing dinner, nearly dying in a theatre, and getting shot at in a baker's yard. Call it a hunch, but there was a reasonable likelihood those four clowns didn't stand a chance.' He looked down at the Temeschwari casualties. 'Where to next?'

'This way,' said Helenus.

The three were sitting outside the city walls, in the public gardens of Holmauer, on trimmed grass beside a round body of water too modest to take the title of 'lake' but much more than a simple pond. The setting moon and twinkling stars were reflected in its still black surface. In the background came the night noises of the creatures in the Imperial Menagerie, discordant, eerie, and oddly out-of-place.

'We were nearly shot for a spoiled loaf!' said Thaddeus, slightly appalled.

'Welcome to the League. *There are rules to this city, break them and the Prince will break you*,' quoted Helenus.

'I thought you didn't like the theatre,' said Thaddeus.

'I love the theatre, but I'm a cicisbeo – I must have seen that play hundreds of times. I've seen that *production* at least a dozen times.'

'I hadn't thought of that.'

Helenus laughed quietly. 'Act two doesn't usually get such a good reaction from the audience.'

'Nothing worth having is free,' said Cassandra, still thinking about the bread. 'But, as the corsairs say, fortune favours the brave.'

Thaddeus harrumphed at the Freeborn heresy but ignored it. 'I assume knowing where to find discarded bread is a useful supplement to the benevolence of the Church of the Little Mother?'

'The Church raises orphans and foundlings and ensures they are educated and placed in an apprenticeship,' said Helenus absently, as if reading from notes.

'And yours was as cicisbeo?'

There was an empty silence.

'I'm sorry, I was insensitive, said Thaddeus.

'Being a cobbler would have been much worse!' said Cassandra gaily and broke the awkwardness.

'Or a *baker*!' laughed Helenus, and the twins started to unload Thaddeus's cargo of loaves.

'I cannot believe you did that!' Thaddeus shook his head. 'Have you no respect for hearth magic? It's as if I had got one of your precious mirrors and popped a big spot or something!'

'Do stop moaning.' Cassandra giggled, making a little heap of bread as Helenus dug in the depths of Thaddeus's hood.

One of them held something to Thaddeus's lips and he opened his mouth to find it filled with a delicious sweetmeat.

'You are very trusting,' said Helenus. 'That might have been anything.'

Thaddeus shrugged. 'It's a knack. You two are very skilled at seeing what is good.'

Helenus and Cassandra looked at each other. 'It's a knack,' they chorused, mimicking Thaddeus's Highborn airs, then fell to laughing. 'And you still haven't asked us "why",' said Helenus.

'The suspense is killing me, but I'm sure you have something in mind.'

Cassandra selected a loaf, sniffed it, broke it in half and held the better half in her mouth. She threw the other half on to the lake. It landed with a small splash and floated, slowly absorbing water. A ripple disturbed the water as something slid through the dark depths. Suddenly a fish broke surface, great scales the colour of old jade and a huge gulping mouth which closed on the bread and dragged it under. The three bread thieves looked at each other with delight and each found a loaf and broke it – excepting Thaddeus, who threw his in whole. The twins' offerings were seized and gulped down, but

Thaddeus's one-ring loaf floated alone. Something nudged it from below, then a truly huge scaled head appeared.

The fish was determined to take the loaf in its mouth, which, although large by any freshwater fish standards, was not quite able to close on the loaf. There followed a protracted struggle of increasing fishy frustration, until the loaf became sodden and broke apart and the giant carp was rewarded for its persistence.

Thaddeus shook his head with wonder. 'I have fought warriors wearing lamellar the exact same size as that fish's scales. Don't go too close – one of those things will have your arm off at the elbow!'

The peal of laughter rang out from the twins, delighted by his reaction, thrilled that he was impressed. One of them held a piece of bread to his mouth and Thaddeus took it. He was past trying to work out which was which, and indifferent anyway. The more relaxed they became, the more they were like a single character, sharing thoughts and finishing each other's sentences.

The bread was gone, and Thaddeus lay back on the grass. 'I actually hate you both.'

'Why?' They chorused.

'Because my hood is full of crumbs and pieces of crust!'

That glorious twin laughter was there again, careless, whole, in the moment, understanding that, in a world of desperate struggle, like food, or sleep, or shelter, joy must be taken whenever and wherever it is available. All three of them knew that, like that discarded bread, the night had been something tainted from which they had somehow extracted goodness.

They lay on the grass, their three bodies making the limbs of a "T". At the centre, Thaddeus could hear the twins' breathing, feel their warmth. The stars sparkled above a few scraps of cloud.

'We were wondering,' said Cassandra, 'who you would have chosen.'

'Considering you are wearing each other's clothes, that is an extremely complicated question, but if you want to know if there is a preference, the answer is no, none whatsoever.'

Thaddeus paused and looked up into the star strewn sky above them. 'In Highguard, we don't have contracts of marriage, or cicisbeo like you Leaguers do, or courtly love like the Dawnish. If people want to be together, then they get together.'

'That sounds rather simple,' said Cassandra.

'Yes, it's like a lot of Highborn things, a piece of simplicity that has taken generations to perfect and is of the hugest value and must be protected with great care.'

He reached out and took Helenus's hand in his right, and Cassandra's in his left, and squeezed them. 'Thank you.'

'Thank you?' queried Helenus.

'For sharing, for showing me your city. It's been a wonderful night. I know…I know you are working, but I would very much like to return the favour one day. As friends.'

'It's been…' began Helenus.

'Fun,' his sister completed the sentence. 'We have had a lovely time too.'

Overhead the constellations silently wheeled, below, the breeze rustled the leaves in the trees. The pond held the night sky like a black League mirror.

IX

Gwin guessed it must be about teatime. She was hungry again, and had a craving for Dutch bar snacks which, sadly, was going to go unsatisfied. *Bratwurst!* Brilliant, the next best thing, in curry sauce with chips and mayonnaise. She rolled off the camp bed and started pulling on just enough in-character kit to get across to the out-of-character area without upsetting anyone. She unzipped the tent door to find a reasonable crowd outside, but luckily no one she knew on any more than nodding terms, in-character or out. She was clear for a dash down to the main drag and out of the game. Thaddeus's habit was something the German larp suppliers called a "duster", and she'd bought it mostly because it was on a special deal. It wasn't really like a Western duster coat, being black wool, and without sleeves, but with a hood. It was more like a cloak, with a small cape over the shoulders. Now, she loved it more than anything. It had been an absolute lifesaver this weekend. She put up her hood and strode down to the main track. Anvil was still madly busy.

Two very small Highborn in tiny chapter surcoats were fighting with larp-safe mock wooden swords and held her at sword point. Gwin put her hands up, then dodged around them and fled laughing. At the track, she passed a merrow, a lineage touched by the magic of the Day Realm. He was of Urizen, from his flowing robes of blues and greens, and had webbed hands, gills on his neck, colourless white eyes, and long, wobbling barbells on his blue face. He looked grotesque, but amazing, and Gwin could only imagine how long the makeup must have taken. She stared, then smiled at him as she walked past. He didn't seem to mind. When she reached the gate, she consciously did the 'one-two-three-and-back-in-the-room' that she knew a lot of players did to break from character. She drew a breath, then joined the queue at the bratty stand.

Suddenly, the merrow was standing alongside, in a parallel queue for noodles. Gwin smiled at him. 'I'm sorry I stared back there, but your makeup is amazing!'

'Thank you.'

They both reached the counter at the same time, ordered, and walked clear of the queues balancing food and cans of drink. 'I'm going to sit on the step by the skip,' said Gwin. 'Are you meeting anyone?'

'I was, but it looks like they got caught up. Mind if I join you?'

They arranged themselves on the wooden step. 'I'm Gwin, by the way. My character is Thaddeus.'

'I'm Zac, my character is Leontius. What are your pronouns, if you don't mind me asking?'

'Gwin is she/her, Thaddeus is he/him. I don't mind if people call Thaddeus "they", because I know they're just being careful and polite – but I am working quite hard to make him convincingly male. And you?'

'Zac is he/him; my character is he/him too.'

Zac snapped his chopsticks apart, rubbed the tips together, and loaded some noodles.

'Blade Runner,' said Gwin. 'I always do that, but I've never seen anyone else do it!'

'I wondered where I picked up that habit. *Too bad she won't live. But then again, who does*?'

'Don't move.' Gwin tucked a paper serviette in Zac's collar. 'You absolutely must not get sauce on that costume!'

'The maker recommends getting some wear on them – she's a player who does commissions. It's amazing the difference having a costume makes when it's been built around your character – like a theatre costume. That said, having sweet-and-sour sauce down the front would be extremely un-Urizen though!'

'I can imagine – about having a costume, I mean. I'm new to Anvil, and I didn't think nearly hard enough about Thaddeus's soft kit. I got all excited about his armour – but unless you do all the skirmishes, you're only going to wear armour for a couple of hours at most.'

'You should commission him a robe or something – something special.'

'I think I need shoulder pads, even double pads, to get his outline right. And I might get some lifts too.'

'Lifts?'

'Foam wedges that go in your shoes to give you a bit more height. If you'll excuse me asking, why do you go to all the trouble of being a lineage?'

'Well for a start, not all the nations are as funny about lineage as the Highborn are – and even then, it's usually briars that get the bad reputation. Lineage is like, like a gift that comes with a curse, or the other way around maybe. Being lineage gives you characteristics you have to bring out in your role-play – so merrow are calm, rational, curious, which fits in really well with Urizen, which is a culture based on magic, reason and Ambition. Sort of High Elves with a bit of Vulcan. I based Leontius around Dr Lazarus…'

'*Galaxy Quest*? I love that film so much! Sigourney Weaver as a character called Gwen – they might have made it for me.'

'There's actually quite a lot of Alexander Dane too.'

'Alan Rickman was just brilliant.' Gwin did the voice. '*That's your problem Jason, you were never serious about the craft.* I can't wait to meet Leontius.'

'He's a questor, a priest who believes the Way is unfinished doctrine and must be examined and perfected.'

'Oh my, that is right up Thaddeus's street. He's a Highborn questioning the Way, which isn't going down well with his fundamentalist Exarch.'

'You should come over to the camp. We've actually got quite a lot of ex-Highborn at the moment. You can see what the Egregore magic is doing to them, turning them into Urizen.'

'I don't really understand all that.'

'Well, obviously the Egregor is the point of contact when you're trying to find out about playing a character in a nation. If you change nations, then the Egregor magic means that you start taking on the characteristics and attitudes of that nation. From a purely mechanical point of view, it stops the nations getting watered-down and keeps them different, because that's what generates the friction that makes the game fun. Like Urizen history, and Highborn history. Both nations have a fanatical interest in history, but Highborns want to use it to illustrate points, support claims – basically do things with it. They will edit it and manipulate it to make sure that it does its job. Urizen want to know what actually happened. To a Highborn, that's just frivolous. Come over to the camp, drink some tea with us.'

'I can't, I'm only wearing half my kit, it just wouldn't be right, especially if I'm meeting ex-Highborn. I'd love our characters to meet though.'

'They can have met on the road on the way to Anvil.'

Gwin thought about it. 'That makes sense. Are you coming to the next event?'

'Yes. Do you want to exchange IC letters in the meantime?'

'Can we do that?'

'Absolutely. We can email, but it's really fun to actually get a written letter too. People go mad with quill pens and parchment and wax seals.'

'Okay, let's do that!'

Gwin was sorry to miss out on the visit to Urizen, but Thaddeus seemed to have enough going on in his life. That thread could wait until the weekend was over. She walked back to the tents thinking how complex Thaddeus's character had become. When Gwin had set him up, she had deliberately tried to make Thaddeus an absolutely typical Highborn, common-or-garden variety. She had, though, been excited to write his back story, and was dreaming up pages of it when Beth told her not to upload it to her character's page, because a back story like that could be more of a hindrance than a help. Beth had made a joke about Highborn newbies always inheriting their father's swords, and hating Druj, and suggested Gwin wait until after her first event. Sound advice, as it turned out.

Now, somehow, Thaddeus had evolved into an irreligious, orc-sympathising subversive who might just possibly end up dating a character from another nation who was so high-lineage he was practically a fish. That just went to show the power of play. It seemed he *had* inherited his father's sword though, and Gwin was intrigued by the real Thaddeus's back story: who was his father who had commanded the company before Lazarus, and how had he come to be killed by the Druj? Gwin was loving this game. She snuck into her tent, stripped off Thaddeus's habit and boots and lay down on her sleeping bag, pulling the faux fur blanket over. It was still light. She huffed and rolled over and dug around on the camp bed until she found her Cath Kidston eye mask.

Thaddeus awoke and tried to remain perfectly still to avoid disturbing the twins. It was pointless, two pairs of brown eyes had snapped open as soon as his had. Perhaps, even before. He solemnly regarded two mops of perfumed black hair. 'Time to get up,' he said. Someone responded with a protesting groan.

He disentangled himself from limbs and bedding and slid down and off the foot of the bed. He stood for a moment to gather himself, then crossed to the washstand and poured water from the ewer into the basin. Turning back, he looked at the bed and the forms of the twins. The bed was warm and smelt of their three bodies. More than anything he wanted to be back there. He splashed the icy water over his body and cleaned himself with a flannel, then towelled himself dry, the rough fabric leaving his body burning and tingling. He selected black hose, tight on the calves and baggy at the waist, gathered with a drawcord, then a high-collared black tunic of thinnest linen. He hopped as he slipped his feet into the five-buckle boots and then shrugged on his habit. One good thing about being a Highborn in the League, he reflected, was that no flamboyant city dweller would possibly want to steal his laundry. He buckled on his shortsword and checked there were a few crowns in his purse, then he quietly let himself out.

Thaddeus had found baths. In the city, everything was to be had, somewhere, for a price, and there were a decent set of baths, near the park and built by Highborn artisans no less. He had washed himself, but he needed to steam, to sweat. Then he would get a shave and a haircut. Then he would see Rodrigo, for the final time.

Thaddeus stopped briefly at the courtyard fountain to make his ablutions, then climbed the stone steps. The door opened, unbidden, as he reached the top, and he stepped into Rodrigo's chamber and lowered his hood. The table was heaving with food, despite the hour only being late morning. The bishop was sprawled in his great chair, borne up by cushions. Helenus and Cassandra were standing on either side of the smirking moneylender, watching Thaddeus, their backs against the uprights of Rodrigo's throne, arms folded, in identical outfits of russet velvet doublets, loose hanging slashed sleeves, dark gold hose and tight knee boots. They reclined against the back of the throne like magnificent heraldic supporters on either side of the broad silk escutcheon that was the bishop.

Thaddeus noted with clinical detachment that on seeing the two of them his heart actually did miss a couple of beats. He was becoming an expert on the physical manifestations of love. He was irritated: irritated that the twins, who, knowing them, as he now did, only crawled out of that ruined bed ten minutes before, could still contrive to look so utterly bewitching, and irritated that after all his careful preparation, Rodrigo had still managed to completely wrong-foot him. He might as well have tripped on the threshold and fallen into Rodrigo's chambers on his hands and knees.

'I thought it would be nice for the three of you to be reunited one last time, for breakfast,' purred the bishop. 'Guardian Thaddeus, it delights me that you are embracing my hospitality with such…enthusiasm. But you will appreciate that such as these do not come cheap. You are running up something of a bill, I merely hope there is enough left to put some tiles on your chapterhouse roof.'

Cassandra stepped away from the bishop's pillowed throne and turned on him. 'What we do in our own time is our business!'

'Indeed?' queried Rodrigo. 'But *are* you on your own time? Or is your time, and everything else mine?' He reached out and pinched her so sharply she cried out.

Thaddeus felt the tide of lethal rage swelling inside him, hoped it wouldn't show, and knew instantly from the triumphant look on Rodrigo's face that it did.

He looked at the twins' worried expressions. 'Helenus and Cassandra have done exactly what you commissioned them to do, have they not? They have fulfilled their duties to the letter.'

Rodrigo steepled his fingers and considered the matter. 'Well…Yes, I suppose they have.' He turned to the twins. '*Go*! Get out! We need to talk without distractions.'

The twins fled, each with a last concerned look at Thaddeus, who kept his eyes on the bishop.

'An old man, lonely and alone, with only his imagination for company, while his…associates…disport themselves. It is almost tragic.'

Thaddeus accepted coffee from a servant and sat in his accustomed place. 'I don't think *imagination* was ever required. I believe you make the most of any opportunity that presents itself.'

There was an uncomfortable silence.

'Are you suggesting I spy at keyholes?' demanded Rodrigo haughtily, his gleaming round face a picture of injured innocence.

'No, of course not,' replied Thaddeus. 'You have plenty of people to do that for you. No, I am *stating* that you spy at spyholes.'

'You knew?'

'Yes. Candle smoke behaves a certain way when there is a draft from a hidden room. I knew it was you because of the way you move.'

'Are you suggesting I am heavy?'

'I don't need to suggest that. I am saying that you are not furtive. Not bold, exactly, but…unapologetic. Shameless even.'

'You knew, and yet…'

'Yes. Here everything is a transaction.'

'You have some Leaguish blood in you, of course?'

'No, I simply give people credit for being who and what they are. You are the Bishop Rodrigo Borges Mão de Ferro di Tassato, the Iron Hand, the Leaguer. I…I don't underestimate that.'

'I thought for a moment you were going to say "respect", but we both would have choked would we not?'

'I have offset my debts where I can, your Excellency. I hope you agree.'

Rodrigo selected a toothpick from a jewelled holder and began to poke it between his teeth. 'Actually yes.' He threatened Thaddeus with the toothpick. 'Don't become arrogant – or any *more* arrogant – but with you gone, I'm not sure what I will do with myself, so to speak.'

Thaddeus winced, then cleared his throat. 'I would ask you a single favour, on my behalf, not that of my chapter, and in the full knowledge of what that means to a Leaguer, under a League roof.'

'Ask then.'

'The twins. Don't hurt them. Please, do not break them – break their spirit.'

Rodrigo gave his barking laugh. 'My poor dear Highborn friend, you have been spun and played. The twins do what they have been taught to do, what they are paid to do. What it is they do for a profession. Do you really think you are the first person to be unbalanced by their pretty faces? No, my friend, to them you are a client of a client, a task, a *job*.'

'Yes. Nevertheless, I am asking you, as a favour to me.'

Rodrigo's eyes narrowed as he regarded Thaddeus. 'By the Virtues, they have you badly. You understand, there will be a reckoning?'

'Yes.'

'Then I hope you consider it was worth it. The boon is granted.'

Thaddeus inclined his head. 'Thank you.'

Rodrigo shouted at his servants to bring parchment and a pen, and then prised one of the rings from the little finger of his left hand. The servant placed a small piece of parchment before the bishop and he took up his pen, dipped it, then wrote an address.

'I don't want you wandering the trods with a small fortune of my money. Take the ring to this man, at this address, and the amount we agreed will be waiting.'

He handed Thaddeus the slip of parchment. Thaddeus read it and his eyes widened.

'You know the place?' asked Rodrigo.

'Yes, and the man. Just around the corner from the chapterhouse.'

'And you had no idea he was an agent of mine?' Rodrigo beamed with delight. 'I would ask you to respect this confidence, and respect that his arrangements with me are strictly confidential. It will serve both our interests.'

Thaddeus shook his head with wonder. 'You constantly surpass yourself.'

Rodrigo held out his jewelled hand imperiously. 'You may kiss my ring – well one of them.'

Thaddeus ignored the proffered hand and bowed from the waist. 'Your Excellency, I look forward to our next meeting.'

'You can't spend the whole weekend hiding in your tent,' scolded Beth, her head inside Gwin's door.

Gwin stretched, rolled off the camp bed, slipped on her wellies and pushed Beth backwards, following her out into the night. 'I guess it's time-out?'

'Yes, are you okay?'

'Really good actually – I've fought in a huge battle, saved a cataphract who turned out to be in on the Military Council, visited the hospital, visited the Military Council, talked to generals, eaten an in-character meal with Varushkans who want me to visit, explored all of Anvil, drank shots with an orc and traded some of my green iron, and agreed to exchange letters with a Urizen questor. Oh yes, and I owe Baz's character a drink for saving my life.'

Beth was impressed. 'Wow! You have been busy.'

'How about you? Come on, don't keep me in suspense, I want to hear *all* about your day.' Gwin wondered if she had always been so adept at deflecting a conversation, or was there just the merest hint of the social graces of those oh-so-skilled twin cicisbeos? No doubt for her, every day at Anvil was turning out to be a school day.

It was very late, but everyone was hyper, and they needed to unwind and debrief around the crackling flames of the fire pit – and there were marshmallows. By being an attentive listener, Gwin encouraged everyone to tell stories – not least because it was really interesting to find out how others had spent their day, and she was learning more about the game every minute. Then the Exarch and Baz appeared out of the dark, still in full costume and carrying their mage staves. 'Sorry, can't stop, I just need to get to my tent and die…,' said the Exarch as she pushed past and disappeared again into the gloom. Baz stopped by the fire pit. 'There was a debate. Gods, was there ever a debate.'

'Ah, Conclave!' said Russell. 'The ultimate test of endurance. Never mind your soppy battles…'

'My hero,' said Gwin, toasting Baz with a pewter tankard of Sainsbury's Dandelion and Burdock. Baz blushed and then blushed even deeper when Gwin told the story of the anti-venom, and Baz's character's heroics on the battlefield.

'It's just what my character's like,' said Baz.

'Yeah well, Adjutant Taliah is going to be buying some drinks. As for me, I'm not sure I'm going to take the field at all unless you're within arm's length!'

Everyone clapped Baz on the back, and they smiled shyly.

Reaction was beginning to set in. People were becoming quiet, yawning. Beth studied Gwin for a moment. 'Well…what do you think?'

'It's exactly like you described, and nothing like I imagined. Thank you for sharing it all.'

'I was worried you weren't enjoying it.'

'It's really draining, and I don't mean that in a bad way – you just really find yourself putting everything into it. I know how the Exarch feels.'

'Bed!' said Russell and hauled himself to his feet.

Gwin wasn't ready to sleep again yet and sat sipping her dandelion and burdock while the fire slowly burned down.

Beth's head was nodding, she looked up and stretched. 'That's me done, I'm turning in.' She stood to go back to her tent. Gwin held her arm. 'Beth, when you're at Empire, do you dream?'

Beth stared at her. 'That's an odd question. No, I'm always *way* too tired. Out like a light!' She freed her arm from Gwin's grip. 'Don't stay up too late, and don't get cold. Sweet dreams.'

'Probably,' said Gwin.

After Beth had gone, she finished the last drops of dandelion and burdock, then went back into her tent and rummaged by torchlight to find Thaddeus's five-buckle boots and his habit. She left the tent, zipped it up and put up Thaddeus's hood, and set off into the night to explore. Play had ended at 1am, but there were still plenty of people still playing in character, and there were lights and activity in the Senate. Anvil had changed its mood once again and was dark, mysterious, great fields of secrets. Gwin flitted along the avenues between the tents, noticing other shadows. She could move like a ghost and people passed her unseen in the dark. Suddenly she missed the twins, she missed Thaddeus too. She went back to her tent, wishing there could be warm bodies against hers. She loved the way Thaddeus held the twins tight, protecting them for the brief hours they were his.

X

Guardian Thaddeus was in the surcoat of his chapter, beneath a gold encrusted embroidered robe. He was wearing his shortsword and bell, and had an elaborate embroidered hood folded across his shoulders. He wore black leather gloves and layered leather bracers. He commanded his own company now, and he moved around the White City as though he owned it. The address Rodrigo had given him was barely yards from the chapterhouse bounds and Thaddeus was angry that Rodrigo had bought the creature that lived there – or somehow held him in thrall – and angrier still that he had to support and conceal the arrangement. He pounded the door with his fist, far harder than was needed.

The door opened, and a ferrety man peered around, looked over Thaddeus's shoulder, and bustled him into the house. The door opened on to a flight of steps, and the ferret beckoned for Thaddeus to follow him.

'It's up here, under guard,' said the ferret.

'Indeed?' Thaddeus's left hand swept back the robe and gripped the scabbard of his shortsword. He eased the weapon free in its scabbard by pushing up the cross hilt with his thumb. There was a landing, with some doors. Ferret tapped on one, then opened it, beckoning with his head for Thaddeus to follow. All Thaddeus's senses were stretched as he tried to determine if he was walking into an ambush. Warily he walked into a small room lit by a window of glass bottle bottoms. The light was greenish brown and diffused. Thaddeus made out a table, chairs and two beds, all mean but serviceable. There was a plain wood box on the table, a disappointingly small box.

There were two figures, guards. It took Thaddeus a moment of bewildered disbelieving recognition to make out Helenus and Cassandra. This time there was no posing, no posturing, the twins exploded across the room and threw themselves at him. He gathered them in his arms, and they all overbalanced and crashed into the wall. Supported by the groaning wattle partition and dusted with plaster they clung to each other, holding each other as tightly as they could manage.

When they had regained their senses, Thaddeus pushed himself away from the wall, holding a twin around the waist on each side. Then he had to let go to dash some tears away.

'Well look at you!' laughed Cassandra. She stepped back and both twins bowed, a courtesy that involved every inch of their bodies; a wide backward step, a sweeping bow from the hips, arms spread, right hand brushing the floor, head bowed, black hair flowing wild.

Thaddeus bowed stiffly from the waist feeling as if his gold embroidered garb was sackcloth and soft leather boots a peasant's clogs. Helenus and Cassandra were so beautiful it actually hurt.

The twins spun him around and investigated his robe making approving noises.

'It is so good to see you,' said Thaddeus simply.

'I think we are on a mission of some sort,' said Helenus. 'We asked Rodrigo if there was a message for you, and he just said we were the message.'

'Does that make any sense?' asked Cassandra.

'Yes, Cassie my darling, it does,' said Thaddeus and smiled. Then he looked worried. 'how long have we got?'

'We can stay here for three days. We must be on the trods on the fourth day,' said Helenus.

'So little time,' said Thaddeus, running his hands through their hair. He shook his head. 'Right, business before pleasure.'

He approached the small box with a sinking heart and reached across the table to slide it towards him. It didn't move, almost as if it was nailed to the tabletop. There was a simple catch, the box was sealed with a wax seal bearing Rodrigo's mark. Thaddeus unfastened the latch and lifted the lid, breaking the seal. Inside there was no pile of sparkling coins, just a piece of folded parchment covering the contents. Thaddeus lifted the parchment, and beneath was a row of gold bullion bars, each near rectangular, with slightly bowed sides. Thaddeus lifted one out. It was absurdly heavy for its size and carried a scatter of League proof marks. Beneath was second row.

Thaddeus unfolded the parchment. There, in Rodrigo's bold script were the words 'Payment in full' and his "R". Everyone in the room had known that the box contained a treasure, but the neat row of shining ingots was still enough to stop all four of them breathing. Thaddeus closed and fastened the box, lifted it on to its side, took a candle from the mantle and dripped a blob of wax over Rodrigo's broken seal. He removed Rodrigo's signet ring from his pouch and pressed it into the wax. He handed the ring to the ferret. 'Ensure this reaches Rodrigo.'

'T-they can take it to him,' stuttered the ferret, handing back the ring.

'If that will suffice.' Thaddeus lifted the box and handed it to the ferret, who looked like he might overbalance. 'Take this to the chapterhouse gate and demand to see the Master-at-Arms. Tell the porter you have urgent material from Guardian Thaddeus. Don't give it to anyone except the Master-at-Arms personally, tell him it's from me, and for the Exarch. Do I make myself clear?'

The ferret nodded nervously and hugged the box to his narrow chest. It took him both hands and all his strength to hold it there.

Thaddeus studied him. 'There are more reasons than I can I possibly enumerate why that box and its contents should not get lost between here and the chapterhouse. I, for one, will be furious, but the bishop, now he really be vengeful.'

'I understand,' said the ferret, nodding wildly.

'Then go.'

The ferret fled down the stairs.

The twins had been watching the exchange with interest. 'It is day, the sun is risen, and we are on the bishop's time. You have a town to show us,' said Helenus.

'Unless, of course, you're embarrassed about it, compared to a place like Holberg,' said Cassandra. 'You know we'll completely understand if you are…'

Thaddeus made a lunge for her, grabbed her, and threw her over his shoulder. Cassandra shrieked and beat at his back with her fists. He ignored her and looked at around the room, noting a scatter of empty dishes. 'You have breakfasted?' He asked Helenus. Helenus grinned at him and nodded.

'Right, in that case we are going to the baths.'

'And after the baths?' asked Helenus.

Thaddeus pondered the question. 'A very late lunch, or possibly early supper.'

'How long do you people spend in the bath?' demanded Cassandra from over Thaddeus's shoulder.

'You are just about to find out.'

'Do we need anything?' Helenus queried.

Thaddeus smiled. 'No, nothing whatsoever.'

'I think I might like Highguard,' said Cassandra.

Thaddeus was anxious to show the twins how the baths provided a centre for the culture of the Highborn, but he need not have concerned himself. The twins understood immediately, and with their almost supernatural ability to win friends, they were soon chattering happily with citizens of every station. Through the cold room, warm and hot rooms, in the plunge pools and sweat rooms, the twins gathered happy noisy throngs voicing advice, and venturing information and opinions. The proprietors of the White City's oldest and most famed bath house quickly appreciated that something special was happening, and ensured the twins, and Thaddeus, were exposed to the very best the bathhouse had to offer.

The supreme moment came when they moved to the area for exercise and massage. It had apparently never crossed Cassandra and Helenus's minds to even carry towels, and the two stood framed by the gleaming marble of the vaulted entryway, holding each other's hands, two innocents abroad, as a profound silence spread across the great busy, crowded, steamy space. The silence held until it was broken by the pop and tinkle of a dropped oil bottle bursting on the stone floor, and even then, for a beat more, before someone scolded somebody, and rushed to sweep up, before any bare feet were injured.

Eager masseurs clustered around the twins and steered them towards the couches. And Thaddeus too. He lay on his front, with warm stones down the curve of his back, watching the twins. They chattered with wide-eyed enthusiasm about anything and everything, without any reticence or self-consciousness, and soon the people around them were doing likewise. Old injuries and pains were described, and the masseurs crowded around offering suggestions. Techniques were explained and tried, oils offered and sniffed and rubbed in. Thaddeus noted with vexation the stab of jealousy he felt when he saw others lay their hands on his two friends, and groaned inwardly, and banged his forehead on the rolled towel that cushioned his marble couch.

An advantage of the twins taking centre stage was that Thaddeus was able to organise the day, still relaxing on his stone couch, by way of a small squad of squires from the chapter, who stood solemnly in front of him to receive their orders, then rushed off on their various errands, bare feet pattering on the mosaic and tile floor of the bathhouse, returning later to confirm that arrangements had been made.

Eventually the three had exhausted everything the baths had to offer. Dressed, and looking and feeling thoroughly scrubbed, rubbed, oiled, and steamed, they were waved off from the bathhouse doors by a great crowd of well-wishers. Helenus's stomach growled, and then Cassandra's did too. 'That was *sooo* nice! But Thaddeus, I have such an appetite.

141

If I don't eat soon, I'm going to have to hunt something down and kill it…' Cassandra rubbed her stomach and looked woebegone.

Thaddeus laughed. 'Just bear with me for one quick visit – I have got us an appointment, and we need to be there as quickly as we can. I promise after that you can eat yourself to a standstill.'

After a short walk, they found themselves in front of an austere black door. It was large, immaculate, and unadorned in a way that suggested that whatever lay behind simply did not need to draw attention.

'What's this?' asked Cassandra.

'A tailor's shop.'

The twins looked at Thaddeus, mystified.

'I thought it might be more comfortable when we visit the chapterhouse if you were dressed in a Highborn manner, and I thought you might enjoy experiencing a different fashion. Your boots and doublets – and codpieces – are certainly drawing attention.'

'You mean dressing like Grey Pilgrims?' laughed Helenus.

'Don't even joke about it. Brother Joel is our finest tailor. He would rather burn himself alive than dress you in sackcloth and a rope belt!'

Thaddeus reached to rap on the door, but before he could do so, it was opened by a mousey figure in a tight black tunic and hose. 'I am Brother Joel's assistant, well, one of them…He is expecting you. Please come in.'

The door let into a large room that was the famed tailor's workplace. The actual floor space was limited, as there were racks and shelves holding rolled fabrics against every wall, mannequins with part-finished outfits pinned over them, rolls and lengths of trim, swathes of furs, and stacked boxes and drawers filled with buttons and beads and fastenings. At the back, lit by a huge window, was a big cutting table. Joel the tailor was sitting cross legged on the table, intently stitching a panel of tiny gleaming beads. He looked up from his work when Thaddeus and the twins entered and unfolded himself, sliding down from the table in the closest Highborn version of the twin's cat-like grace. He was not tall, but he was thin in a way that made him appear long.

'Joel,' said Thaddeus with a nod.

'Thaddeus,' replied the tailor. The two were clearly on informal terms.

'Thank you for seeing us at such short notice.'

Joel silenced Thaddeus with a gesture and walked to the twins and around them. He took their arms and walked them away from Thaddeus, towards the cutting table and the back of the shop. Thaddeus moved out of the way, to let the great man and his assistant get on with their job. Joel's expert eye minutely examined the twins' doublets, and approved, particularly noting what their tailor in Holberg had done that flattered their body shapes. 'Off!' He snapped. 'Take them off!'

He swung a wheeled ladder along the wall, then climbed up to rummage amongst a stack of bolts of black cloth on the topmost shelf. He meant the doublets, but he wasn't very clear, and the twins had just spent the whole day in the bathhouse. By the time the master tailor had found the cloth he wanted, descended the ladder with the heavy bolt under his arm and turned to face the twins, they were standing in the middle of his shop quite naked.

Thaddeus was leaning against a wall at the front of the shop, vastly amused. The mousey assistant was standing slack jawed. It did Joel great credit that there was only the merest flicker of surprise, then his eyes started to sparkle. He looked like a sculptor who has woken up to find a twenty-ton block of flawless marble standing in his workshop.

An elegant dance of measuring and note-taking followed, with Joel and the twins apparently communicating subliminally, as few words were spoken. Joel's assistant never quite regained her composure, broke her pencil, dropped her notes, and got quite seriously scolded by the great man.

As suddenly as it all started it was over. 'Dress yourselves,' said Joel dismissively, waving a hand. He turned his back on the twins and walked over to Thaddeus. 'Tomorrow morning. I don't know when, nine o'clock perhaps. To the chapter house?'

'No,' said Thaddeus, 'The town house. And the other items?'

'All in hand.'

They turned to watch the twins, who were pulling on their long boots.

'Thank you for your help,' said Thaddeus.

For the first time ever, he saw the master tailor's mask of imperturbable superiority slip. 'No,' murmured Joel, 'Thank *you*. It is very seldom that one has an opportunity such as this. I commend you on your exquisite taste.'

Somebody's stomach gave a great growl and Joel put his hands to his ears, as if a marching band of orc drummers had just transited the shop. 'Out!' he shouted. 'Out, out, out! How can I possibly work with this noise and distraction?' He waved a long finger under Thaddeus's nose. 'And you! Feed them at once! Call yourself a host? The shame of Highguard!' He tossed the comma of hair that hung over his eyes, waved his hands in the air in a gesture of helplessness, then hustled Thaddeus and the twins to the door with impatient irritation and ejected them into the street.

The door snapped shut behind them.

'What just happened?' said Helenus.

Thaddeus smiled. 'You made another friend.'

'He doesn't exactly tout for business,' said Cassandra, looking at the blank façade.

'He doesn't need to; he has a waiting list about a mile long. Two miles, in fact.'

'And we just jumped it,' said Helenus.

'About as completely as is imaginable.'

Cassandra's stomach growled again. She glared at Thaddeus.

'Follow me,' he said. 'Now we eat.'

'What is Joel making?' asked Helenus as they walked.

'I honestly have no idea.'

Around the corner was a building with a shaded courtyard full of tables. 'Oh, this is *nice*!' said Cassandra.

But that wasn't where they were going. The proprietor rushed out to meet them, and bustled them through the building, past a sizzling kitchen that nearly stopped the twins in their tracks, and into a courtyard at the rear where fountain played into a shallow pool, and a single table stood under a pergola laced with green vines. Members of the proprietor's family were already placing small earthenware dishes on the table as they took their seats, and more followed. They were eating Highborn style: sun-dried tomatoes, cheeses, salads in

145

olive oil, breads, cured meats, green and black olives, fresh herbs, fruits, hummus, yoghurt. Thaddeus lifted a napkin from a basket of rolls and tossed one to Helenus, who caught it, yelled, and juggled it from hand to hand; it was scalding hot from the oven.

'Better check it's fresh!' laughed Thaddeus.

The roll bounced across the table. Helenus took up a flask of wine and splashed it into their beakers. He raised his cup. 'The bread thieves!'

'The bread thieves!' they chorused.

Thaddeus had imagined he was giving a tour of his city to a pair of ultra-sophisticated cicisbeo from the heart of the League but found himself apparently confronted by two half-starved street urchins. The twins were in rapt concentration, lost in a world of their own, standing up to lean across the table, hands flying over the selection of dishes and piling food on their plates. Thaddeus was famished after the better part of a day in the bath house, but it was surely physically impossible for Helenus and Cassandra's trim bodies to accommodate the amount of food they were gathering up. He wondered if they were going to start shoving it down the front of their doublets.

The urgency gradually ebbed, faltered, and was replaced with a contented silence, broken only by a burp from Cassandra.

'Sorry.'

Thaddeus was interested to note that the twins' enthusiasm had been more about experimenting – trying a bit of everything, then trying everything with everything else – than the sort of determined gluttony of bishop Rodrigo. They had certainly made up for a day in the baths and their time on the road, but at least they would still be able to walk.

'You Highborn live well,' said Cassandra.

'It's not what we were expecting,' said Helenus.

'Steely-eyed orc hunters in grim towers living off porridge and religion?'

Helenus smiled. 'Something like that.'

Thaddeus shrugged. 'There is an element of that. It depends on the character of the chapter, and the location too – think of the differences between the cities of the League. The White City is old, I mean ancient. When we go to the chapterhouse, I'll show you the baths we found.'

'Oh good, *more* baths,' said Cassandra tartly.

'We don't actually use these ones…'

'Even better.'

'They are hundreds and hundreds of years old, maybe thousands.'

The twins' eyes met, and they subsided in laughter.

'I'm not spinning you a tale,' said Thaddeus. 'The buildings around the chapterhouse are old, but those are built on top of even older buildings, and those on yet more – and then, under all that, a huge bath house, ruined of course, but with the waters still running. It's fed by the only hot spring in the White City, and all anyone knows is it's really, *really* old. The Exarch has archivists swarming all over it, but unless they find an inscription or something, all they can do is guess how old it is.

The point is, people have been doing what we did today in the same place, in the same way for maybe fifty generations. After all that time, things get sort of *refined*, pared down. There probably was a time five hundred years ago when people didn't feel they had had supper unless they'd been served a peacock in its skin and feathers – but would this meal have been better sprinkled with gold leaf, or served on silver trenchers, or in a sugar paste model of the Sentinel's Tower? I suppose we try to get to the essence of things, the bit that really matters. At least that's what the Exarch is trying to do with this new chapter.'

Thaddeus shifted uncomfortably, realising he had been going on a bit. 'Sorry!'

'No,' said Cassandra, 'It's interesting, it sort of makes sense of what we are…'

'Observing?'

There was a silence. 'Yes,' said Helenus.

Thaddeus smiled. 'Good!' He reflected for a moment. 'I think a few weeks of Highborn living might do Rodrigo rather a lot of good.'

Mention of the bishop's name cast a shadow, as if the sun had suddenly dipped behind cloud, but the twins were too skilled to allow the mood to break.

'If no one is having that last piece of buffalo cheese, it's mine,' said Helenus.

Thaddeus picked up the smooth white cheese and popped it into Helenus's mouth. 'Your appetites are most gratifying.' He licked his fingers, then reached across the table and took the twins' hands. 'Let's go and find you somewhere nice to stay.'

They all stood, and Thaddeus chivvied the twins through the house and out the front, while he stopped and settled-up with the proprietor. He counted crowns from his purse, then walked out into the courtyard to find the twins had joined a party of elderly Highborn. Cassandra was standing at the head of the table learning a drinking song, while Helenus was about halfway down, receiving an exposition on baked fish. Thaddeus took their hands and physically dragged them away, while their new friends protested noisily, and the twins waved and apologised and promised to return.

'You would be more than welcome to stay at the chapterhouse,' said Thaddeus, 'but you might find it all a bit straightlaced. It's also quite busy at the moment. We have this town house for visitors we want to keep at a bit of an arm's length.'

'Charming!' exclaimed Helenus. 'Some welcome!'

Thaddeus blushed. 'I'm sorry, that came out all wrong. It's quite pretty, and…and it means I can have you to myself.' He looked guilty and mortified. 'I will take you to the chapterhouse, of course. I'll get you to meet everyone.'

'Paragons preserve us, you can be *so* sweet,' said Cassandra, shaking her head.

They were standing in front of a tall narrow doorway in a wall of old stone. The two leaves of the door were of wood, faded to grey, its grain etched by time. The iron fittings were rust-browned but polished with use. Thaddeus turned the two rings of the door handles and pushed the leaves apart. The twins peered over his shoulders.

Beyond the door there were plain columns, arches and walls of mellowed stone, and ancient stone planters crammed with herbs, in a courtyard that had trapped the evening sun. A fountain with four spouts played into a tiled pool, a flight of stone steps led to a long balcony and the upper floor. The walls were covered with climbing shrubs that were a cascade of flowers – except on the south-facing wall, where small trees stretched their fruit-laden branches fanwise over the warm stone. There were bright plumaged songbirds fluttering in and out of the flowering creepers, and at the edge of hearing, fine glass wind chimes stirred in the soft evening breeze. The twins gasped and pushed past Thaddeus with a skip and scamper as they burst into the courtyard, racing around, exploring, sniffing perfumed blossom, wondering, laughing, and catching ice-cold, crystal-clear water in their cupped hands and splashing it into their mouths.

The housekeeper was coming down the steps, an elderly woman in a plain habit with a pile of folded linen in her arms.

'Guardian Thaddeus.'

Thaddeus bowed his head. 'Sister Ruth.'

'I've freshened all the linen in the bedrooms. Will you be staying too?'

'Thank you. Yes, I will.'

Sister Ruth examined Thaddeus from her vantage point on the stairs. 'I've turned down the bed in the Great Chamber. I'll tell the ground staff to warm the bath in the morning.' She looked at Thaddeus and the twins. 'Not too early, I'm guessing.'

She descended the steps and walked to the doorway and paused. The old housekeeper looked from Thaddeus to the twins and back again and mischievously held her ground for a moment or two longer than was strictly necessary while he fidgeted and started to blush, then she turned and walked away, throwing her head back with a delighted laugh.

Thaddeus closed the doors, barred them, and stood with his back against them for a moment. Then it was a race, the three scrambling pell-mell up the stairs. More than anything they needed to divest themselves of the absurd encumbrance of belts, boots, clothes. It was frantic, tearing at each other's clothes and their own. Laces that knotted were snapped, hooks ripped out. They left a trail up the stairs and along the balcony. The Great Chamber had a Great Bed, and by the time they reached it they were naked and running like deer.

They all knew that the next few hours would be the measure against which every night of their lives would be judged. The location would never again be this perfect: the setting sun, the warm breeze stirring the long muslin drapes in the windows and carrying the scent of herbs, the lazy hum of insects, and the birds calling in the vines. And they would never again be this young, this beautiful. Thaddeus's love for the twins was complete, total, and unreserved, and they loved him to the maximum extent they could love anyone who wasn't their twin. Nothing that burnt so fiercely was destined to last long, and that made it even more important to seize the moment. To seize every coming moment.

In the muzzy reaches of the night, the Gwin Weyve-Ross personality emerged. Gwin was no prude, but her experience of lovemaking was limited to the barest minimum needed to qualify. There had been *that* time, then the time after that, which they both hoped would be better, and the time after that which confirmed it wouldn't, and that they would have to go their separate ways. There had been quite a lot of online searches, extended conversations with hungrily hopeful friends to determine what it was that floated her boat, readings of some of the more invigorating classics, and some viewing of various content, but nothing had prepared her for what just happened. She knew she had been exposed to the game at a truly stellar level, and nothing would ever be quite the same again.

From her very privileged viewpoint, she had learned a mass of lessons. The first was that the best of what happens in bed is the magic of building trust, and intimacy, of bonding and sharing. The second was that if each participant sets aside all thoughts of their own gratification and concentrates on pleasuring their partners, then a most satisfactory time can be had by all. She was struck, from where she was watching, by how much effort was required on the part of the men, and for a relatively slender return – especially considering how much fuss they make about the subject. She reflected that, if men received anything like the payback women did, probably very little work would ever get done. On the subject of which, her conscious presence meant that Thaddeus was, literally, in touch with his feminine side, and the night had had signal benefits for Cassandra, who was presently sprawled on her front, tangled in a sheet, one arm over the side of the bed, breathing quite noisily through her mouth. The building might have fallen down around her, and she would have slept through it.

Gwin watched and felt as Thaddeus gently freed himself from Helenus and slid off the bed. He crossed to the washstand and took out the chamber pot from the cupboard under the ewer and put it on a chair. The whole process still held an enduring fascination for Gwin, who was gratified to note that this time Thaddeus's first-shot accuracy was spot on, but less impressed when he crossed to the window and emptied the contents of the pot into the street below. The Weyve-Ross persona fluttered, disapproved, and faded.

Thaddeus replaced the pot and crossed to a settle, lifted the seat, and removed a folded blanket from the linen chest below. He shook out the blanket and carefully laid it over

Cassandra, softly kissed her cheek, then climbed over her, back into the bed and gathered a sleepy Helenus into his arms. He lay on his back stroking Helenus's hair, listening to his breathing, feeling the beat of his heart, and staring at the ceiling above, until sleep reclaimed him.

XI

Gwin woke up and studied the roof of the tent. Gwin, Gwin-as-Thaddeus, or Thaddeus? She blearily wondered. A quick examination confirmed that it was one of the first two options, and also confirmed that she was busting to pee. She had been dreaming about it, it was a miracle she hadn't wet her sleeping bag. Gingerly she crawled out of the bag and pulled on her blue floral wellies with the magenta soles and Thaddeus's habit, then carefully crawled out of the tent.

'Good morning,' said Beth.

'Gotta pee.'

'What?'

'I think she's gotta pee,' said Russell.

'Where's the nearest honey wagon?' demanded Gwin.

'Nearest what?' asked Russell.

'Out-of-character area,' said Beth, and Gwin was on her way in a blur.

'What did she call it?' asked Russell.

'Honey wagon,' said Beth. 'Film speak – honey wagons and gulley suckers. Honey wagon is the mobile toilets, the gulley sucker's the thing that empties them, like a little truck with a big steel tank on the back.'

'You seem to know an awful lot about this.'

'Yes, well, contrary to popular opinion, my job doesn't consist entirely of getting selfies with Brad Pitt. Actually, it's getting two hundred cast and crew and all their equipment onto a location, keeping them relatively warm and dry, getting them fed and watered and carting away the...waste. More practical than glamorous, although, thankfully, I hire the people that do all those jobs, rather than do them myself.'

'Is that what Gwin does too?'

'No, she does a lot of research and stuff.'

Gwin had her hood up to discourage anyone who might be tempted to stop her and talk. If that happened, she would probably fill her wellies. She had already decided that if there was a queue at the ladies she would be straight in the gents. People did it quite often, but she had always been a bit chary. Now, well, what happened behind the door with the little man on it was an open book. She considered herself a member – so to speak.

She need not have worried, there was no queue, and better yet, the crew had just been in and the place was spotless. On the back of the door was a notice about the morning's battle, which nations would be fighting, and which would be 'monstering' – dressing as orcs to provide the enemy. There was also some extremely funny graffiti, which the maintenance team had thoughtfully decided not to clean off.

'Better?' asked Beth, attacking a supermarket fruit salad with a pink plastic spork.

'Much,' said Gwin and made a couple of dance moves. She reached up, hands together, as if about to dive, then crossed her legs, bent at the hips and touched her toes, then stood with legs apart and placed her hands flat on the grass.

Beth eyed her, loaded spork halfway to her mouth. 'What are you doing?'

'Nothing,' said Gwin, and did a perfect League bow, a step back, bending from the hips, head down, her right hand brushing the grass.

Beth looked at the tent. 'What have you been up to? Have you got someone in there?'

Gwin straightened up, bit a piece of mango off Beth's spork and kissed her on the forehead. '*Pastime with good company, I love and shall until I die*', sang Gwin spinning on the toes of her wellies.

'You are actually scaring me.'

'Time for a bacon roll. I always say…'

'No!'

'It helps…'

'No, I'm warning you.'

'To start the day…'

'I have a bottle of water, and I'm not afraid to use it.'

'With-something-greasy-inside-you!'

'You were warned. Wasn't she warned?' And Beth pursued a shrieking Gwin around the tents, hurling water at her.

Replete with breakfast and slightly damp, Gwin crawled back into her tent to find Beth had followed her in.

'You see? All on my own!'

'You're being very strange.'

'Beth, you were totally, *totally* right, larp agrees with me. Wish I'd started years ago, nothing like a bit of immersion. I'm going to take a power nap before the battle. If I'm not up in an hour and a half, send in a search party, I may need Haribos orally, heavy dose.'

Beth shook her head and backed out of the tent, zipping up the door. Gwin lay down on her camp bed, pulled a blanket over, slipped on the Cath Kidston eye mask and put her earphones in. She turned up her music and wondered what Thaddeus and the twins were up to.

Something was tapping on Thaddeus's forehead and somewhere a bell was ringing insistently. Thaddeus opened his sleepy grey eyes and found himself looking directly into Cassandra's wide brown ones. It was Cassandra tapping on his forehead.

'There's a bell,' said Cassandra, helpfully.

Somehow all three of them were now crammed together under Cassandra's blanket. Thaddeus groaned, sat up, pulled the blanket off the protesting, resisting twins, wrapped it around himself, and set off for the entrance. The sun was already well up, and the stone flags of the courtyard were warm under his feet. There seemed to be discarded clothes all over the place. Blearily he unbarred the doors, muttering, 'Coming, I'm coming!' Outside was a delivery boy holding three large boxes. There were two big flat ones and one deep square one, and he was almost entirely hidden.

'For Guardian Thaddeus, with Brother Joel's compliments,' shouted the boy from behind the boxes.

Thaddeus took the boxes and put them inside the doors, he reached for his purse to give the boy a tip, realised he was wearing only a blanket, and was momentarily at a loss, then he went to one of the espalier fruit trees, picked a juicy apple and threw it to the boy. The boy caught it, examined it, and said, 'A peach too I reckon.' Thaddeus laughed and picked

157

one, throwing it at the boy who caught it one-handed grinned at Thaddeus and ran off.

Thaddeus climbed the clothes-strewn steps with the pile of parcels, losing the blanket along the way. He didn't have enough hands.

The twins were on the balcony. 'Is there a problem?' asked Helenus.

'Not at all. A delivery.'

'From Brother Joel?'

'Yes.'

They sat on the bed and Thaddeus handed out the flat boxes. Each twin's box contained a simple black cassock. They took them out, shook them out, and then held them against themselves. 'You had better try them on,' said Thaddeus.

Joel had made each of them a cassock with a high standing open collar. The cassocks were closed with a long row of tiny buttons in seven groups of seven, that stretched from collar to hem. Each button was a tight little knot of the same fabric he had chosen for the body of the garments, the finest black wool, smooth to the touch, but woven with a pattern that shimmered in the sunlight. It wasn't one of the angular patterns preferred by the Highborn, or the floral patterns of Dawn, but something complex and swirling that seemed completely right on the two Leaguers. That had been what the master tailor had been rummaging for when the twins surprised him. It was a brilliant choice, but Joel probably might have waited half a lifetime for the right opportunity to use it. The buttons were for effect, and the cassocks fastened with hooks and eyes. The linings were fine linen and black silk, the skirt of each cassock flared slightly from the top of the leg, and the hem was just above the ankle. There was a panel under the opening at the front, and a deep pleated vent behind, so the long garments would not hinder the twins' movement in any way, but swirl as they walked. The twins tried them on and danced around each other exclaiming and posing.

'Oh Thaddeus, they are beautiful!' said Cassandra.

'Why don't you people have mirrors?' said Helenus.

'For pretty much the same reason you have lots of them, powerful things. I think there's one in the next bedroom though.'

The twins were out of the door before he had even finished speaking, and he caught up with them jostling each other in front of a tall mirror. The quality of the work was stunning – it must have been a long night in the tailors' quarter, and Joel must have called in every favour he was ever owed. The black cloth fitted each twin as if it was painted on, more than that, the cut accentuated their body shapes – their narrow waists, the flair of Cassandra's hips, Helenus's shoulders. In their simplicity, Joel's two outfits were the purest genius.

'What should we wear underneath?' asked Helenus.

Thaddeus shook his head. 'Nothing, unless you want to ruin the lines. I think Joel made those to fit like gloves, you'll probably need to skip breakfast – and keep your breathing shallow.'

He had the square box with him, and opened it, pulling out two pairs of charcoal grey suede ankle boots. He compared them sole-to-sole, tossed the larger pair to Helenus, and offered the smaller one to Cassandra. 'Single buckle fighting boots – thin sole,' he teased. The boots did indeed have one buckle behind the ankle, and enough of a heel to lengthen the leg and neaten the stride. The twins pulled them on.

'How do we look?' They lined up for inspection.

Thaddeus was lost for words. Even with bed hair, no makeup and outfits experimentally thrown on, the result was stupefying. 'I think I may have to buy Joel a drink when I next see him. In fact, every time I see him for the rest of his life. Now, take the clothes off please.'

The twins looked at him questioningly. 'Aren't you being a *little* bit greedy?' asked Helenus.

'It's bath time.'

'What again?' said Cassandra. 'We only bathed yesterday.'

'Yes, which means in Highborn terms you are due for another.'

The twins rolled their eyes and the three of them began removing Joel's beautiful clothes, which should have speeded the process up, but instead led to further delays. It was some time before they wandered down the stone stairs towards the town house's own bathhouse, which was at the front of the building, near the courtyard doors. Inside, there was a great tiled tub filled with steaming water; cloths and towels had been laid out, and keen razors and tweezers. The twins were punctilious about shaving, Thaddeus didn't have much body hair, but Helenus and Cassandra made him feel like some shaggy mountain beast, and he was minded to follow their example. He tested the water and winced.

'Hot?' asked Helenus.

'Chop a few carrots in and they can serve us for lunch. I think the boiler has been going for hours.' Thaddeus let cold water run into the huge bath.

'What are these?' asked Cassandra, pointing to a tray full of differently shaped and coloured bottles.

'Bath oil. Choose one.'

The twins sniffed at the bottles. 'I recognise this,' said Helenus.

'You ought to, they're all made in Sarvos. Highguard isn't exactly known for producing perfumes.'

There was an investigation, a dispute, a squabble, a reconciliation, and a choice. 'This one,' said Cassandra, holding out a bottle.

'Tip it in,' said Thaddeus, who was easing himself into the bath.

'How much?'

'All of it.'

Thaddeus stirred the oil into the bath, and the water turned milky. He sniffed the fragrant steam. 'Good choice.'

The bath could comfortably hold ten, but the three had, as usual when they were together, managed to fit themselves into the smallest space possible. Helenus was lounging back against the side of the bath, with Thaddeus lying against him, Helenus's arms were crossed over Thaddeus, Cassandra was sitting on Thaddeus's lap with his arms around her waist. The hot perfumed water was up to their chests.

'We've been wondering…,' said Helenus.

'Why are you called Guardian Thaddeus?' finished Cassandra.

'It's…' Thaddeus tried to find the word. 'An honorific – it means a veteran.'

The twins burst out laughing. Cassandra grabbed Thaddeus's chin. 'I'm looking.'

'No grey hairs,' said Helenus, peering closely. 'And that's ridiculous, you're the same age we are.'

'Two years older, *actually,*' said Thaddeus with the haughty dignity of a ten-year-old squire. He shook off the twins. 'It means I have completed my military service, in my case in the Army of the Seventh Wave. I served in the last part of the campaign to drive the Druj from Reikos.' A shadow passed over Thaddeus's face. 'Interesting times. Character building, I suppose you'd say.'

'But you only must have been…' began Cassandra.

'In my teens. Yes, a guardian is also a type of soldier, line infantry, mail hauberk, greaves and vambraces, strong enough to join a shield wall, but not heavy infantry. The heavy infantry are the cataphracts – they used to be heavy cavalry back before all the horses died out. They're the ones in full plate – *cap-à-pie* as the Asaveyans say. The light infantry, skirmishers and scouts, the stealthy ones, we call the unconquered.'

'I've seen you trying to be stealthy, that's definitely not you,' said Cassandra. Thaddeus splashed her.

They were all out of the bath. 'Lightly perfumed is good, smelling like a Dawnish flower festival, not so good.' He stood the twins back-to-back.

'What are you doing?' asked Cassandra, worriedly.

'You're going to enjoy this. Very bracing.' And he up-ended a big pail of ice-cold water over them. The twins yelled fit to raise the roof.

The twins fixed each other's hair and their makeup, which was lighter than their usual League look. Thaddeus was beginning to understand why they could look so immaculate so quickly – it was a lot easier when there were two of you, identical, and so attuned to one and other as to be practically telepathic. He dressed in his surcoat, under the gold embroidered robe, and over his thin black tunic and hose. He pulled on his five-buckle boots, buckled his long belt, and then finished off with his iron circlet and bracelets. No bracers or gloves, he was off duty. The twins shrugged on Joel's cassocks, and then slipped on their dark grey boots. Cassandra and Helenus looked perfect, a beautiful compliment to their Highborn hosts. Thaddeus fished in the bottom of the square box and pulled out a flat, folded paper parcel. He opened it and took out two circlets, finest gold, thin flattened wire that joined at the front in an overlapping motif, like two slim leaves, with a tiny sparkling stone set where they crossed. At the back, the circlets were fastened with ribbons of some yielding fabric that would hold them firmly but comfortably in place. Thaddeus unwound both circlets, and holding one in each hand, held them out to the twins.

Cassandra put her hand to her mouth. 'Oh Thaddeus, those are just beautiful!'

'The finishing touch, we Highborn like our circlets.'

He held them out for the twins. 'No, you put them on us,' said Helenus, and Thaddeus did.

'We never gave you anything when you visited Holberg,' said Helenus.

'Yes, you did actually. My most precious thing.'

The twins looked at him blankly. Thaddeus reached under his robe and slid a small pouch around from the back of his belt to where they could see it. It was leather, the kind that might hold a few small coins. Thaddeus untied the drawcord and took out something that looked like a fragment of stone, craggy, dark brown, and slightly polished from being in the pouch. Helenus reached out and took it from him. 'Bread?' he said, wonderingly. It was dried up, as hard as rock. Thaddeus nodded.

'Did you find it in your hood?'

Thaddeus laughed. 'No! That's the piece one of you put in my mouth when we were beside the lake. Well, half of it. I ate the other bit.'

'Thaddeus, that's ridiculous,' said Cassandra. 'We'll get you something lovely when you next visit!'

'I don't want anything else. When I'm missing you two, I get that out of the pouch, and there we are – the bread thieves.'

Gwin lifted up her eye mask, Beth was in the doorway of the tent. 'You need to go and get monstered-up for the battle. This time, when you get out on the field, you'll be an orc!'

'Yes, I rather suspect I will,' said Gwin worriedly. 'I'm not sure I'm quite ready for that,' she groaned. 'I really don't think I can, I'm totally exhausted! I know you're supposed to monster if you've fought, but I was thinking, I'll miss the battle next time, and just do the monstering.'

Beth frowned. 'The battle rule is "play one, crew one", you're not supposed to do that, but I guess it's alright if you keep your word. Does this mean you want to come back again?'

'Absolutely!'

'Okay, well you recharge your batteries. Do you need anything?'

'You couldn't pass me a packet of Starmix could you?' said Gwin, pushing her luck from the cosy comfort of the camp bed.

Beth scrambled into the tent and tossed two mini-packets of sweets to Gwin. 'I sometimes wonder why we are friends.'

'Because I love you and love you.'

'Yeah, right.'

'What are you doing now?' asked Gwin, helping herself to Starmix and offering the packet to Beth, who selected a gummy egg and a ring.

'Getting set up for the Exarch's meeting. We've been putting up posters and handing out flyers, it's a really good way to meet people around Anvil, if you want to join in later. We've also got to steal some benches and things from the other chapters, because there's going to be quite a crowd.'

'Okay, well just let me nap for a bit and then I'll maybe join you later.'

Beth shook her head, pulled Gwin's eye mask over her eyes and scrambled out of the tent, zipping the door behind her.

XII

Thaddeus and the twins walked through the open gates of the chapterhouse. The porter smiled, nodded an acknowledgement, and watched them with friendly interest. The twins were magnificent, statuesque, like pillars of black marble. Beside them, in his embroidered robe, Thaddeus felt gaudy, and wished he had worn his travelling habit. Helenus and Cassandra had changed their posture and walk. No longer the wide-legged swagger of the bravo, but not tripping steps of a cleric either; they strode like Highborn, straight-backed, confident and purposeful, arms at their sides, looking as if they had been in the chapterhouse every day of their lives. As the three of them passed, people stopped and looked up from whatever they were doing, eyes followed them, as did a barefoot gaggle of small children, who trailed them at a discreet distance and noisily shushed each other and scrambled over one and other to get the best view from around a corner or through the legs of a statue.

Thaddeus had in his head a planned a tour of the chapterhouse, but that was arrested by the arrival of the smallest squire he had ever seen. He knew she was a squire because she was wearing the squires' off-white hooded tunic, with the chapter sigil on the breast. The tunic, which looked to have a year or so of growing room in it, was tied around the waist with a cord, from which hung a rosary. Although she only came up to Thaddeus's belt buckle, the diminutive squire carried herself with the dignity of a general; she halted in front of Thaddeus and the twins.

'Guardian Thaddeus, the Exarch will see you and your guests in the cloister garden directly.'

Thaddeus inclined his head. 'Thank you. Whom do I have the honour of addressing?'

'I am Squire Abigail,' said the child. 'And these are?'

'Cassandra van Holberg and Helenus van Holberg,' said Thaddeus with formality, indicating the twins.

Squire Abigail bowed from the waist, her arms remaining stiffly in line with her upper body, so the effect was almost doll-like. The twins bowed to Squire Abigail in the same manner, but with rather more grace. 'Follow me,' she said, and set off, her sandals slapping on the polished stone of the chapterhouse floor.

The Exarch was seated on a stone bench in the cloister garden, deep in conversation with a secretary. There were books and rolls of parchment, even a map of the Empire. When he saw the four approaching, he concluded his business with the secretary, who gathered up the various papers and left, with a polite nod to Thaddeus.

Squire Abigail led Thaddeus and the twins to where the Exarch was seated. 'Exarch, Guardian Thaddeus, Cassandra van Holberg and Helenus van Holberg,' said the girl, gave one of her stiff bows, took two steps backwards, turned and sped away.

The Exarch studied Thaddeus and the twins. 'Cassandra, Helenus, I am delighted to meet you, it is always a pleasure to

167

entertain guests from Holberg – quite my favourite home from home.'

Thaddeus took a knee, bowing his head. The twins gave their elegant version of a Highguard bow. The Exarch stood, took Thaddeus's arm and bade him stand. 'Please my friends, you have me at a disadvantage, said the Exarch, looking at the twins. 'I had not expected you dressed so – you look more Highborn than the Highborn. I hope our fashion is not too uncomfortable?'

'We could not be more comfortable,' said Helenus. 'Highguard is constantly surprising and delighting us.'

'There may be trouble though,' said Cassandra.

The Exarchs brow furrowed. 'Trouble? How so?'

Cassandra looked about. 'It's a secret, but we're planning to capture Brother Joel and carry him off to Holberg.'

The Exarch shook his head. 'Fighting talk! Citizens would never yield the White City's foremost sartorial resource. An outrage on that scale might tear apart the very fabric of the Empire!'

'Perhaps we might borrow him?' suggested Helenus.

'Just for a couple of decades,' said Cassandra.

The Exarch burst out laughing. 'I understand you are here to tour the new chapterhouse? Well, please allow me to be your host for a short while. The extent to which Guardian Thaddeus has applied himself is the talk of the city, do rest yourself in the garden Thaddeus, I will get one of the squires to bring you some refreshment, you must need to regain your energy.'

The twins laughed, and the Exarch took them each by the elbow and steered them out of the cloister garden. 'I hope you will recognise a few conceits I have included in our new home that remind me of Holberg – no one here can spot them at all! I also *insist* you tell me everything that is happening in Holberg – I want *all* the news.'

Thaddeus liked the cloister garden. Unlike the courtyard of the town house, it was not sun-baked, but cool. It had a purposeful, business-like feel. It existed to provide herbs for the kitchens, and – most importantly – the infirmary. Although, like the rest of the chapterhouse, it was very new, mature plants and even small trees, had been imported and the garden had become quickly established. Thaddeus fell into conversation with a sister from the infirmary called Theia, who was cutting herbs and laying them carefully in a shallow basket on her arm. In a sunny corner, a group of scholar-pilgrims were sitting together, poring over crisp new copies of the Exarch's book, pointing out key passages to each other, underlining in pencil, and arguing excitedly about the meaning of the Exarch's meditations on Virtue. His lotus-eaters he had called them. Thaddeus studied one portly Varushkan occupying most of a stone bench and decided that some of them needed to go easy on the lotuses.

Thaddeus was finishing an apple tea when a squire appeared and told him he was required in the chapter refectory to join the Exarch and guests for lunch. Thaddeus thanked the boy and handed him his glass, straightened his robe, and set off. The new chapter was rapidly gaining a formidable reputation for the quality of its table, with a proud and enthusiastic kitchen staff, constantly spurred to new heights by one of the founders, a former-Freeborn, who brought Brass Coast variety and cosmopolitan, pan-Empire cuisine to the chapterhouse. These things matter more than people credit, and opportunities to dine at the smart new chapterhouse, to see and be seen, to talk business and politics and religion, were eagerly sought. The twins were seated at the high table with the Exarch, and had, as usual, drawn a crowd, but the happy acclamation, Thaddeus noted, was not universal. There was a cohort of senior members of the chapter, in fact *all* the senior members of the chapter, keeping their distance, with angry faces, engaged in urgent, heated conversation. Some of them saw Thaddeus walk in, and their looks were daggers.

Thaddeus washed, then took a plate and selected a few items from the cold table, wondering if anything there was a lotus, and if he'd recognise one if he saw one. He vaguely thought they were water lilies, which didn't sound very appetising. He took a typically Highborn selection of a few cold meats and some salads, then joined the twins. As he did so, the Exarch excused himself and got up from the table. 'Duty calls I'm afraid. I will see you all after lunch, in the cloister garden?'

The twins happily chatted with new friends, finding out anything and everything about this new, thriving chapter, and the ferocious Loyalty the Exarch inspired. Thaddeus watched, adding the occasional comment, and just happy that they were happy. They all finished the meal with tiny glasses of Brass Coast coffee, served by squires. It was strong enough to float a spoon on, and hot enough to melt it. There were pastries, but Thaddeus took two pieces of Freeborn delight from a platter and put them on the saucer beside his steaming glass and licked the powdered sugar off his fingers.

'I didn't know you had a sweet tooth,' said Cassandra.

'I don't usually, but this stuff – I can't resist it, I mean, literally, I would sell my soul. It goes right back to childhood.'

'Well come on, tell the story!' said Helenus, stirring his coffee.

'You know the big annual festival in Highguard is the Day of the Dead?' The twins nodded.

'Well, when I was small, we would have delight – we called it lokum. The children had to line up in age order, and you had to show your hands were clean and say your catechism – the Seven Virtues – then you could take a piece out of the box. If you got it wrong, you went to the back and had to queue up again. The pieces were shaped like little skulls and dusted all over with powdered sugar. It was very festive.' Thaddeus paused, remembering. 'I always took mine and ran off as quickly as I could, I'd climb up into the loft over the ox stalls, where it was warm from the animals, and take my time eating it. If I didn't hide away, the chances were that one of the bigger children would take it, and I would have to wait a year for another piece!'

Cassandra held up one of the pieces of delight to Thaddeus's mouth. 'Bite!' He did, and sugar spilled on his chin, and they all laughed.

'That night, when the torchlight procession came past, I would wriggle through a whole forest of legs to get to the front of the crowd for the best view. Each chapter marching past in silence, hoods and veils, bells, draped icons and reliquaries, standards and banners. What a sight! I still get chills when I hear a bell tolling and a slow single beat on a drum. And I always think of that ripping sound the flames make when the wind catches the torches…They would read out the names of the year's fallen, and we could stay up late to listen – after midnight even.' Thaddeus shook his head wonderingly. 'And they say Highborn don't know how to celebrate!'

171

'I had no idea you were such party animals,' said Cassandra carefully.

The Exarch joined them again later, when they had finished their coffee and were once more in the calm of the cloister garden, deciding what to do next.

'I'm afraid I have dull tidings,' said the Exarch. 'Guardian Thaddeus and I are required for a meeting of the chapel, the governing board of this chapter, this afternoon, and we will need to take some time to prepare ourselves.' He smiled at the twins. 'We will have to forgo your company for a few hours. However, I understand your time with us is short, so I have arranged access to all the sights of the city – the Great Bell Tower and so forth – and we have given some of the junior squires the responsibility of hosting you until supper. I hope that meets with your approval?'

'We have trespassed on enough of your time,' said Helenus.

'Nonsense, you have been the most charming company, but I'm afraid our younger siblings may wear you out a bit, so I will not invite you to dine with us tonight, I will ensure the housekeeper has a meal for you at the town house, and Guardian Thaddeus can host you.'

The twins responded with gracious bows. The Exarch clapped his hands. 'You must be getting on. Squire Abigail will keep order.'

A file of young squires appeared, led by Abigail, who looked severe. Cassandra put her hand out to the girl, who regarded it with suspicion, then looked about, uncertain of the correct conduct. Deciding it would not be appropriate to offend the guest, she diffidently took Cassandra's hand.

'Your tunics are so smart!' said Cassandra. 'That is the chapter sigil, isn't it?'

Abigail nodded and looked up at Cassandra. There was a melting between them. Abigail tightened her grip and moved closer to Cassandra.

'Where are we going?' asked Helenus, and the squires started jumping up and down and shouting.

'My respect for Rodrigo increases by the moment,' said the Exarch as the twins were born away by the flock of squires.

'He is everything you described and more.'

'Am I correct in understanding he has an agent in the White City?'

'He has an agent forty yards from the chapterhouse bounds.'

'And that is just the one we know of.'

'Yes.'

The Exarch pondered for a few moments. 'We cannot have been of any special interest to the bishop until your visit – and yet he had an agent to watch us. Imagine what it must be like to attract his interest.'

'He watches very closely,' said Thaddeus, with feeling.

'Such a useful thing,' mused the Exarch. He guided Thaddeus towards a stone bench. There was a chessboard, pieces arranged mid-way through a game.

'I forget – do you play?' asked the Exarch.

Thaddeus shook his head. 'No, I could never remember all the different moves.'

'You preferred to practice with sword and shield, as I recall.'

'Yes.'

The Exarch sat on the bench and looked at the game. 'It's a game of conquest and sacrifice. You have to be willing to make sacrifices to win. That is how I know that if I play Rodrigo, I will beat him. He is greedy, he needs to hold on to as much as he can grasp. I am Ambitious, I can lose some to win all.'

'Ambition is a Virtue,' said Thaddeus absently, 'so that must be good.'

'Indeed. You lead a company of soldiers; you know that sometimes a leader has to ask people to make sacrifices – for the greater good?'

'There isn't a person in this chapterhouse who wouldn't give their life for you in an instant.'

'Yes, we Highborn are very quick to lay down our lives. A noble death in battle, a quick spin around the Labyrinth, then rebirth and another shot at perfection. Regrettably, unless one applies oneself in this life, it is going to take a very great time to achieve perfection. Also, the greater good requires all manner of sacrifice, not just the noble ones. From all of us.'

The twins were being dragged along the cloister with several children tugging at each hand like a team of Suaq sled dogs, twins and squires were laughing.

The Exarch watched the Helenus and Cassandra. 'They are a powerful asset.'

'Yes, Rodrigo holds them close.'

'As, by all accounts, do you.'

Thaddeus felt his cheeks burning. 'They are my dear friends.'

The Exarch studied Thaddeus's face. 'Surely, they are anyone's dear friends?'

'So people never tire of reminding me,' said Thaddeus wearily, he smiled ruefully. 'Even Rodrigo.'

'That was very candid of him.'

'Oddly, considering the circumstances, this is an enterprise characterised by a surprising amount of candour.'

'So, everyone has warned you, even their master, and you still give them your heart. And you *have* given them your heart, have you not? It seems to me you are walking into an ambush, despite every conceivable warning.'

'They give me something I never found anywhere else.'

'I hardly dare ask, knowing the legendary skills of the cicisbeo, but I fear I must.'

Thaddeus stared up at the blue sky above the crisp new stones of the cloister. 'They make me happy.'

'Happy?'

'Not a very Highborn word, is it?'

'Presumably, every satisfied client can say the same thing. You realise this sounds foolish, vain, and selfish?'

'I think they do love me.'

'And you believe that, in spite of every rational argument to the contrary?'

Thaddeus smiled. 'Isn't that the definition of belief?'

'Belief is important. Important to me – I believe the concept of the greater good, I believe in human destiny, in the primacy of the Empire, in the Sevenfold Way. You believe in the love of two cicisbeo.'

'Yes.' Thaddeus paused for a moment. 'I also believe in you.'

'I am gratified to be in such exalted company.'

'I am in love with two Leaguers, you are in love with one. You are probably the only person in Highguard who might understand how I feel.'

'Yes, actually I do. But I also appreciate the risks – the pulls that can drag us from the path, which in your case are double.'

'I am going to ask you something,' said the Exarch, 'and I want you to consider very carefully before you answer.'

Thaddeus nodded.

'Did you bargain with Rodrigo?'

'You know I did, I got us the funds you wanted.'

'That is not what I meant. Did you personally treat with Rodrigo?'

Thaddeus thought for a minute, and then described the spyhole and the secret room. He was surprised how much something that seemed coldly rational in Holberg sounded sordid in the brightly lit cloister garden in Highguard.

The Exarch considered. 'So, you were able to spend time with the twins, ensure they were safe from Rodrigo because they had completed their mission, and gratify the bishop, thus squaring all accounts. Are you sure you don't play chess?'

Thaddeus shook his head. 'I did the best I could.'

'And you consider that you are square with Rodrigo, that you don't owe him a reckoning?'

'Yes.'

'Really? Because if you do, then you have a commitment that transcends all other loyalties, and that means that you cannot be trusted; that *I* cannot trust you.'

'Yes.'

'And this latest three nights of bliss in the town house? Is that a repayment or a down payment?'

'By the time Cassandra and Helenus left the bathhouse they knew practically everything they needed to know about the White City, most of what they needed to know about Bastion, and probably more about Highguard than the national assembly. I exaggerate, but you understand my point. They are on a mission. Guardian Thaddeus's dented, dizzy reputation is an important distraction that prevents people thinking too deeply about what the two pretty and companionable Leaguers are up to.'

'And that is a good thing?'

'Yes. If we are to gain and keep his support, Rodrigo needs to be confident, and that means he needs to understand as much as possible about us.'

'That is going to make him a dangerous ally.'

'Yes, but Rodrigo can never stand for the Throne Imperial, or even get near it. He needs you.'

They sat silent for a few minutes. Thaddeus stirred the gravel path with his boot. 'Do you remember, when we were young, before we were squires even, the children had a game, a rag ball on a rope attached to a stick in the ground. You kicked or hit the ball and it spun around the stick?'

'Yes. They still play that.'

'One day I came upon you standing holding the stick, rope and ball. You had your back to me; you didn't see me. At first, I didn't understand what you were doing, then I realised that you were using it as a battle mace, a morning star, swinging it against imaginary enemies you were facing alone. You were making huge swings: they must have been the biggest orcs – trolls even. You made one great swing that spun you quite around and you saw me. You looked at me, threw down the

177

stick and ran away. You thought I would mock you, tease you, tell the other children.'

'And would you have?'

'No. I wanted to fight at your shoulder.'

The Exarch picked up a chess piece and turned it in his hand. 'I wish you had not told me that story.'

'I'm sorry, I didn't mean to embarrass you.'

'You didn't, at least not in the way you mean. Come, we have a meeting of the chapel to attend. You understand that as Exarch and potentially as Throne candidate I cannot be associated with this arrangement with Rodrigo, despite its importance to everything we are trying to achieve. *Because* of its importance to everything we are trying to achieve.'

'Yes. I understood from the outset.'

'This meeting will be uncomfortable.'

'Yes.'

'You will not have my support.'

'I understand.'

'Do you? It is very important that you understand.'

'I understand.'

XIII

The Exarch parted from Thaddeus before they reached the chapel, where the meetings were held that governed the chapter. Thaddeus found himself entering the room alone, there were voices that stilled to a hostile silence as he entered. He took a seat and sat with his hands in his lap, eyes on the table in front of him. Some of the other members of the chapel meeting greeted him coldly, others openly cold-shouldered him. On the long table were a small bell, a minute book with ink and quill, and Rodrigo's box, which stood open, in the centre. One layer of ingots had been lifted out and placed beside the box.

The Exarch entered, took his seat at the head of the table, cast his eyes over the meeting, then lifted and rang the bell to bring the chapel to order. 'We are called to this extraordinary meeting of the chapel to consider the matter of Guardian Thaddeus and his...ah...treasure.' The Exarch gestured towards the gold bars. 'It appears that Guardian Thaddeus has, on his own initiative, travelled to Holberg, engaged the services of a Leaguish moneylender and secured a very considerable sum in gold in the name of the chapter.' The room was filled with voices. The Exarch waved his hand, and when that didn't still them, rang the little bell. 'Guardian Thaddeus, kindly explain yourself.'

Before Thaddeus could say anything one of the other chapel members slammed her fist down on the table. 'Thaddeus has put the chapter in debt to Rodrigo – the one who calls himself "the Iron Hand", that creature, that usurer. I move that we return the gold to Rodrigo immediately, preferably with Thaddeus's head!'

There was a hubbub of voices and the Exarch let the furious senior members of the chapter rage unchecked. He judged the moment and rang the bell again. 'Thaddeus, what have you to say for yourself?'

'Rodrigo is not a usurer...'

'No?' shouted the sister.

Thaddeus said quietly, 'A usurer lends at outrageous rates of interest. That gold is a loan repayable over five years at six percent interest, which is a fair rate. Not over-generous, but fair. The sum is sufficient to complete the construction work in the chapterhouse, in particular the Great Dorter – the guest and pilgrim accommodation. This will enable the chapter to increase both its revenues and influence much sooner than we had planned. In addition, there is an amount to provide a fighting fund to support the candidacy of our Exarch for the Throne Imperial.'

A stunned silence held in the room. 'And does Rodrigo know what his money is supposedly being spent on?' asked the Exarch quietly.

'Yes.'

The meeting exploded into chaos. The Exarch rang the bell again and again, to no avail, and had to resort to pounding the table with the butt of his dagger before some semblance of order prevailed.

'There are a number of very serious matters for examine here,' said the Exarch. 'I will not have this meeting descend into disorder. Do I make myself clear? We will approach this in a methodical fashion, firstly, the matter of the chapterhouse...'

'Exarch, with respect...surely...' began one of the chapel, then stuttered to silence under the Exarch's implacable gaze.

'All this' – the Exarch waved his hand to indicate the chapterhouse – 'has been achieved through our own resources and the benevolence of the wider community of chapters – a bequest here, a donation there. There is no doubt that, over time, we will eventually complete the chapterhouse, with the unstinting support and generosity – charity even – of other chapters, to whom we are most beholden.'

'And now we can complete the chapterhouse sooner, and on our own resources,' said Thaddeus.

'On Rodrigo's resources!' shouted one of the chapel.

Thaddeus shook his head. 'Rodrigo has advanced us funds against the earnings the chapter will make from welcoming more visitors and pilgrims. He has examined the figures, and agrees they are reasonable. He has not asked for security.'

'I am gratified that Rodrigo thinks so highly of our financial potential,' said the Exarch drily. 'So, let us consider. We now have in our possession sufficient funds to complete the guest complex with immediate effect. However, they were not requested by the chapter, and the matter was not discussed around this table. We can, of course, explain to Rodrigo that there has been a misunderstanding, that one of our senior members acted without any authority on matters outside of his jurisdiction. We could come clean, ask the bishop to take back his loan. I do though feel that it might make the chapter look disorganised and poorly governed; this new chapter of ours might well be something of a laughingstock in Highguard, in the League, and throughout the Empire.' The Exarch mused for a moment. 'It may be simpler and less injurious to our reputation to take the money, complete the buildings, and keep this embarrassing episode to ourselves.'

The chapel members looked gloomy; many had their heads in their hands. 'There is no alternative,' said one. 'We have to take the money.'

'Thanks to what he has done to us!' shouted another, pointing at Thaddeus.

There was a murmur of agreement.

The Exarch looked weary; he pinched the bridge of his nose. 'It is one of the founding principles of this chapter that it is governed by *this* body, at *these* meetings. The Exarch is simply the figurehead, the mouthpiece, a focus for the chapter. Therefore, chapter siblings, esteemed members of the chapel, I need to lay this decision before you. I will accept whatever determination you make. Will the chapter accept this money, understanding that by doing so we are committing to complete the pilgrims' and scholars' lodgings in the shortest possible time, so that we can service the debt?'

There was a long silence, then someone said 'Aye' and there was a chorus of ayes. The Exarch leant towards the secretary. 'Let it be recorded that the motion was unanimously carried, and that chapel recommended to the Exarch that the loan be accepted.'

The Exarch allowed a silence. He balanced his dagger on his fingers, toying with it. 'Now we come to our second matter, and the one that affects and concerns me most directly. At one time or another, almost all the esteemed members of this governing chapel have prevailed on me to stand as candidate for the Throne Imperial.' The chapel members looked at each other, trying to recall who had suggested the Exarch stand, and who had not yet demonstrated their loyalty and trust in their leader. 'I have, of course, laughed the matter off, pleading my youth, my relative inexperience – some might say innocence – of Imperial politics, the pressures of establishing our new chapter, and my immersion in my studies of the Sevenfold Way. Yet, if I am to understand you correctly Thaddeus, you informed Rodrigo, a Leaguish moneylender, that I would stand for the Throne Imperial?'

'Yes.'

'A possibility that has only been discussed in the most general terms, and then only within the security – the sanctity – of this room?'

'Yes.'

'Hang him!' came a cry.

The Exarch struck the pommel of his dagger on the table. There was silence. 'Perhaps you would like to explain to me – and to the governing members and founders of this chapter, your thinking. If "thinking" is the right word.'

Thaddeus considered, then spoke quietly, 'Empress Lisabetta was a most capable and respected head of state. Her demise means that there will be a rush to fill the vacant Throne. None of the candidates will lack Ambition, but they may be less well-endowed in the other Virtues. We may be on the threshold of a time of chaos that could fracture the Empire. It is often said that the best candidate is the one who least wants the job – because they understand what it entails.

I am not aware of a League candidate, and even if there is one, it is inconceivable that the other nations would accept a second Leaguer, cementing the League's hold on the Throne. Inevitably, the League's influence will now begin to fade. However, the Exarch is engaged to a Leaguer, and a member of the late Empress's House, no less. In the absence of a Throne, a consort is a very attractive proposition, of the sort the League understands perfectly – which is why their marriage contracts are so important to them. This means that the Exarch, who might seem to be an outside candidate for the Throne, will be able to call on the support of both Highguard and the League, and that changes the complexion entirely.'

'Thank you, Thaddeus,' said the Exarch. 'I'm sure we are most edified by your grip on the intricacies of Imperial politics.' The Exarch idly spun his dagger on the tabletop. 'The late Empress – I believe we must call her that, despite the circumstances of her demise being rather vague – the late Empress was business-like, capable, extremely hard-working, and skilled at maintaining the unity of this Empire of ours, which we all know is, in truth, a fragile thing. As you say, I am betrothed to a member of the late Empress's House, and I had the honour of meeting Lisabetta on a number of occasions. She will be sorely missed.' There was a nodding of heads around the table.

'I'm afraid I have been too busy to pay any more than scant attention to the matter of candidates for the Throne, no more than is commensurate with my responsibilities as your Exarch.' He paused and collected his thoughts. 'I gather that of the various individuals who have declared an interest, there are two clear frontrunners. The first of these is a Dawnish earl, you all know whom I mean. A flamboyant character from a flamboyant nation, a nation with a rather different interpretation of the Sevenfold Way to our own, and a culture of glory and courtly love. As incumbent on the Throne, he would certainly usher in a colourful and dashing era. Perhaps that would be a good thing after the probity of Lisabetta.' There was a murmur of disapproval, heads were shaken.

The Exarch went on. 'There is, I am told, another strong candidate, Ambitious and capable, and he is an Imperial Orc…' He was interrupted by a hubbub of voices. He raised his hand. 'I am young, and inexperienced in such matters. The Imperial Orcs are valued friends and courageous fighters for the Empire. Perhaps this *is* the time to place our Empire, indeed the future of the human species, in the strong hands of an orc.'

Halfway down the long table a bulky figure pushed back his chair and stood; an old silver-haired warrior, scarred by war and now twisted by age. He slammed the flat of his hand on the table with a crash that made the Exarch's little bell jump. 'Exarch, with respect – and I do mean this with the greatest respect – you are, as you say, young. Perhaps you don't understand the impossibility of what you speak of. We cannot, we *will not* be vassals to an orc.' He stared at the Exarch. 'This will *not* be permitted, not now, not *ever*!'

The Exarch nodded. 'Yes, I see, I understand. Thank you for making that clear to me, for explaining. This is why I rely so heavily on the chapel's council. I defer to your experience. I don't know where I would be without your wise heads and sage council.'

The old warrior took his seat. The Exarch paused and bowed his head, massaging his temples. 'Once again, I fear Guardian Thaddeus's rash actions have forced our hand. I must declare my candidacy, as Thaddeus said I would, or let it be known that I am not interested and allow the Throne to pass relatively uncontested to either our Dawnish friend, or this formidable orc.'

'Shame!' said a voice.

'Disgraceful!' shouted another.

The Exarch stilled the room with a gesture. 'Let me understand this correctly. It is the decision of this meeting of the chapel that I declare candidacy for the Throne, that is what you are asking...telling me to do? Do you understand the enormity of what you are demanding of me? Do you understand that I will need to lean on your unstinting support, your absolute Loyalty, if we are to work this thing? We will need to gather support across all Highguard. We will need to ensure our senators understand where their best interests lie, and the Synod, Conclave and Military Council too. And we must persuade our visitors from the other nations to do the same when they return to their homes.'

The Exarch paused, musing. 'Perhaps you are all right, perhaps it *is* time to return Highguard to its historical place as the leader and defender of the Empire...' His slim figure at the head of the table looked fragile, already weighed down by the responsibility being thrust towards him. He hung his head. A bearded mage pushed back his chair and stood. He was tall and thin, of changeling lineage, with the antlers and pointed ears of his kind, there was too a sparkling wildness that came from the Summer Realm. 'Exarch you have my complete support – with every drop of blood and every fibre. I am yours!'

'And me.' One-by-one each member of the chapel stood, many with tears pouring down their cheeks, conscious of the load they were placing on their young Exarch, and anxious to support him in any way they could. Eventually only Thaddeus remained seated, his hands still in his lap, his eyes still fixed on the table in front of him.

'Thank you, my friends – my dear friends. Let your decision be noted in the minutes – that the chapel prevailed upon the Exarch to declare candidacy for the Throne, and he dutifully committed to do so.'

The Exarch's voice was barely more than a whisper. He made a small gesture for them to sit. 'Now,' he said, raising his head, and fixing Thaddeus with a penetrating gaze. 'I have one last question for Guardian Thaddeus, Why Rodrigo, why the bishop?'

'Yes, why him?' came a shout.

'Rodrigo is a relatively small lender by League standards, and he is on the fringes of League society…'

'With good reason!' shouted the heckler.

'Rodrigo has sufficient means and borrowing from him does not place the chapter in thrall to any of the great houses of the League. Furthermore, whatever his character, he is a Leaguer, and Loyal, and therefore recognises the advantages of having a Leaguer as imperial consort. It is a mutually beneficial and strictly business arrangement.'

There were snorts of derision, and there was ironic laughter. 'Oh, come on Thaddeus!' shouted a guardian. 'Rodrigo bought you. He bought you with those playthings – those sissieboos. You've been made to look a damn fool – because that's what you are!'

'It's pronounced kick-a-bey-o,' muttered the Exarch irritably. He waved his hand. 'Enough! I have heard enough.' He paused in thought, then addressed Thaddeus, 'Your conduct has severely compromised the chapter and left this august body with a number of serious challenges to resolve. You have demonstrated a failure to comprehend the collective nature of decision making in this chapter of ours and acted completely beyond your responsibilities and competence. These are most serious transgressions.'

'Throw him out!' shouted a member.

'Hang him!' shouted another. There was a chorus of approval.

The Exarch held up a hand to still them all. 'I will take into consideration your previous service to the chapter, and the fact that your actions, although wildly misguided, were probably motivated by good intentions. We all must learn from this, and in a way, I feel responsible, I should never have allowed this to happen. Henceforth, the actions of officers of the chapter will be more closely monitored through the office of the Exarch, to protect them from making dangerous and foolish mistakes.

You will be stripped of your offices in the chapter and banned from holding any chapter post for a period of five years. As soon as Rodrigo's ah...emissaries have left, you will rejoin your company – in Therunin, is it not? I recommend that you keep your visits to the chapterhouse to the minimum necessary for the smooth running of your company, and for chapter administration. Now please leave us, we have a great deal of serious business to discuss.'

XIV

The town house felt like home. Thaddeus pushed open the doors to see the twins in the courtyard, barefoot in simple tunics. They looked up and rushed to him and he hugged them against him.

'Those are nice!' He said, looking at their tunics.

'They are so cool and comfortable,' said Helenus.

'We went to see Joel,' said Cassandra, 'and he gave us these. He was so pleased to see us in the cassocks he made.'

'I bet he was just delighted when you burst into his shop with a hoard of screaming children.'

Cassandra shook her head. 'They were so good – I mean *really* sweet. Abigail wants to write to me and come and visit us in Holberg.'

'That would certainly be an education for her. She is the Highborn's Highborn at the moment, I think the League will be a real eye-opener. Thank you for visiting Joel – did you see the sights?'

Helenus laughed. 'Oh yes, we have *really* explored the White City. How was your meeting?'

Thaddeus's face clouded. 'Challenging. Do you mind if I bathe? I need to float for a bit.'

'Do you want company?' asked Helenus.

'More than you can possibly imagine.'

They lay in a tangle of limbs on the big bed. Their wet hair had left the pillows damp, but the evening was warm and still and they didn't mind.

'Do you want to talk about the meeting?' said Cassandra.

Thaddeus shifted between the twins. 'The chapel – the senior members of the chapter who make all the decision – are furious with me, because I placed the chapter in debt to Rodrigo.'

'I can understand that,' said Helenus.

'Then they decided they had no choice but to take Rodrigo's gold and use it, and the Exarch reluctantly decided he had no choice but to accept their advice and stand for the Throne. Then I was disgraced, stripped of my titles and posts, and told to stay away from the chapterhouse.'

'You're joking,' said Cassandra. She saw the expression on Thaddeus's face. 'You're not joking, are you?'

'No.'

'That's dreadful!' said Helenus. 'You have only ever acted with the best interests of the chapter. I could tell them!'

'They say Rodrigo bought me with you two.'

Cassandra was concentrating, her expression serious, her brow furrowed. 'Thaddeus, when we showed you Holberg – you said you had never been there before.'

'That's right, it was my first and only visit.'

'So, a soldier who is usually busy fighting orcs somewhere…'

'Husks, in Therunin, at the moment.'

'Them – suddenly gets it into his head to go to a city he has never been to before and borrow a huge sum of money from someone he doesn't know, without telling the rest of his chapter…' she shook her head, confused, trying to see the picture.

'Go on,' said Thaddeus with a small smile. He tucked a strand of hair behind her ear. 'Keep working at it. You've done better in a few moments than a room full of pompous Highborn managed in an afternoon. The whole chapel have decided I'm mad, or bad, or both.'

'But you're not either of those things…You *must* have been told who to see by someone who knows Holberg, and knows, or at least has heard of Rodrigo – and told how much money to ask for. How would a soldier know all that?'

Thaddeus smiled. 'No, we are quite stupid.'

'That's not what I mean, and you know it! When you first met Rodrigo, you told him your Exarch didn't know you were there. Was that true?'

Suddenly as she was talking, Thaddeus pictured Rodrigo's smirking face, and heard him saying, 'He *is* sharp, isn't he?' and he felt a prickling sensation of horror, and his throat tightened. He knew he must suddenly be sweating. 'Are you asking me as Rodrigo's agent or my dearest friend?' he asked, trying to control his racing pulse.

'It's a conspiracy Thaddeus – and neither Rodrigo nor your Exarch could be seen to be approaching each other. They needed someone to appear to force their hand. You're the only person who knows how all the parts fit together. Oh, Thaddeus,' said Cassandra, eyes wide. 'You're in terrible danger!'

'From where?' He could hear the blood pounding in his ears. He could hear Rodrigo saying, 'There will be a reckoning.' He could hear his beloved Exarch saying, 'I want you to consider very carefully before answering.' Thaddeus looked up at the ceiling, and a sort of serenity came over him. He was, he knew, just a chess piece. Loyalty was a Virtue, so too was Ambition, but love wasn't – unless you were Dawnish. Perhaps, he reflected, he should have applied a little more Vigilance, it certainly seemed that the other players had.

'From everywhere,' said Helenus slowly.

'Everywhere?'

They kissed, and Thaddeus lay back with a wry smile.

'What's funny?' asked Helenus.

Thaddeus shook his head. 'Cicisbeo are a source of enduring fascination outside of the League. There are all sorts of stories. One is that they will never kiss you on the mouth.'

Cassandra was pensive, tracing a pattern on Thaddeus's chest with her fingertip. 'That's amateurs,' she said.

'How so?'

'You get people who come to the cities to make their fortune and end up doing whatever it takes to put food on the table and a roof over their heads. They call themselves cicisbeo because it sounds better and is a recognised profession. Some of them do that. It makes them feel business-like, professional, separate. The thing is, every time they turn their heads, they remind the person they're with that they are just a meal ticket, passing trade, a few coins in a purse, and that is the exact opposite of what it is to be a cicisbeo.'

Helenus rested his chin on Thaddeus's chest. 'A cicisbeo will make someone feel that they are at the centre of the world, that they are special.'

'That they are loved?'

There was a profound silence. It was as if some dizzying gulf had opened under them. Cassandra sat up; her hand flew to her mouth. 'Oh Thaddeus! We do love you – truly we do!'

'Every day someone reminds me that you are professionals and tells me that I am being a fool to give my heart to you. The Exarch did it – even Rodrigo did it.'

Cassandra welled up and started to cry. 'Rodrigo! I hate him so much. He poisons everything!' She made to stand. 'We never should have come here! We must go, right now!'

Thaddeus held her wrist and pulled her back down. 'How is that going to help my darling? I told the Exarch you two did something that nobody else has ever done for me – that you made me happy. If you go, you will make me very sad.'

Cassandra was sobbing, her face in her hands, Helenus was lying with his head resting on Thaddeus's chest. 'We can never prove to you that we love you,' he said.

'No.'

'Because anything we do or say, people would say "well they were bound to say that", and nothing will be proven.'

Thaddeus ran his fingers through Helenus's hair. 'I know. But do you understand that I never asked for proof, and I never will? All I can tell you is I love you both. I don't mean I'm in love with you – although I am, but that is a giddy, selfish, hungry thing. I mean I care, I really profoundly care, from right deep down in the centre of me.'

'We know you really do love us,' sobbed Cassandra, her face slick with tears.

'How?' Thaddeus smiled and kissed her. 'The clothes, the circlets?' he teased.

Helenus shifted against Thaddeus. 'They were lovely, but people have been giving us pretty things since we were little bigger than those squires. No, it was because you kept the bread.'

Thaddeus pulled Cassandra down against him, and Helenus put his arm over her and started trying to sooth her. Thaddeus kissed their hair and watched, wondering how many times in their lives Helenus that had done that, and wondered if his heart would burst with his love for the twins.

'Rodrigo said I was a client of a client, a task, a job.'

'You're not a job!' Cassandra was crying like a child.

There was a pause, then Helenus quietly said, 'Yes, you are.'

Cassandra gasped and tried to pull herself out of Helenus's embrace. Thaddeus held her against them both.

'I know,' said Thaddeus quietly.

'But that doesn't mean we don't love you.'

'I know that too.'

They lay still. Cassandra's breath came in great shuddering gasps. Thaddeus could feel the twins' tears wet on his skin.

After a while Helenus said, 'We do love you.'

'Yes,' said Thaddeus. 'I truly believe you do.' He held them both as tightly as he could, burying his face in their hair, breathing them in. 'And when you have to choose, protect yourselves and each other. Do that for me.'

XV

It was morning, the third day and the twins' last day in Highguard.

'I'm going to find us some food,' said Cassandra, she slid off the bed and picked up her tunic.

'What will you do?' Helenus asked Thaddeus after a while.

'What I have been told to do – rejoin my company in Therunin.'

'I don't even know where that is.'

'It's Navarr territory, to the south of Highguard. Marshy, full of etterspawn and vallorn, and everyone coughing up green lung. At least, the local orcs are friendly. Well, fairly friendly.'

'Sounds delightful.'

'It isn't. But at least it isn't here.'

Cassandra appeared in the doorway holding a laden wooden tray. 'Help! No, seriously, *help*! I'm about to drop all this.'

Thaddeus rushed to her and lifted some clattering cups and bowls from the tray. Helenus reached out from the bed. 'Pass it to me.'

There was yoghurt, a loaf of fresh bread, scalding hot Freeborn coffee, a jug of cold milk, a pat of golden butter and a big comb of honey.

'At least, Sister Ruth loves us,' said Helenus.

'Everyone loves you. It's me they want to hang,' said Thaddeus, breaking some hot bread.

'We were wondering…' began Cassandra. 'Might we stay here today?' continued Helenus.

Thaddeus laughed. 'I was going to ask you just the same thing!'

They were like naughty children, they took the mattress off one of the beds, carried it to the balcony, then dropped it through the pillars into the courtyard, then ran down and threw themselves on it, feeling the sun and the warm breeze on their bodies. They made love with a wild, desperate gaiety. They splashed and played in the big tub, and when they were hungry, they went to raid the kitchen and discovered Sister Ruth had let herself in and quietly left platters and dishes of delicious food on the cold stone shelves of the pantry, and two jugs of chilled red wine with fruit chopped in, and a fresh loaf beside the embers of the stove, wrapped in a cloth. They made a picnic on the kitchen table and fed each other olives and cherry tomatoes and told of their different worlds and discovered all those symmetries and coincidences and similarities that people find when they are together and lost to love. And then it grew late.

When the twins packed the three of them were like strangers, polite, brittle, making inconsequential small talk. They knew these last few minutes and hours were precious, but the sadness was too big to ignore. Eventually they climbed into the big bed, but instead of collapsing into each other's arms, they lay apart, staring up, each with a tumbling turmoil of thoughts. Helenus broke the silence. 'We were thinking...'

'We should go away, the three of us,' continued Cassandra.

'Where were you thinking we should go?' asked Thaddeus.

'The Brass Coast,' said Helenus.

'Aren't the Freeborn Highborn who got tired of Highguard and went away where they could live their own way?' asked Cassandra.

'More-or-less,' said Thaddeus, 'I'm not sure that's exactly how the archivists describe it, but you have the gist. We tend to get on fine as long as we keep our distance.'

'Exactly!' said Cassandra, triumphantly.

'We could hire ourselves to the corsairs,' said Helenus.

'The corsairs?'

'Yes!' Cassandra was excited, eyes wide and bright. 'We can all three fight and you've commanded a company.'

'And we can sail,' added Helenus.

'You can't!'

'We can actually.'

'Astounding.' Thaddeus shook his head.

'We have a little money,' said Cassandra, 'and we could earn more, and get our own ship. The egregore magic would work on us, and we would become Freeborn, but I think the way we are, we would become Freeborn pretty much straight away. With new names and everything, no one would remember our old selves ever existed...'

And together the three wove a dream and embroidered it with so many details that they almost believed it might come true: that there really was a place where they could run and hide themselves and their secret and be free of the people who controlled their lives, whose reach had no limits, who would stop at nothing to rule their world. Weariness overtook Thaddeus, his eyes became heavy, and he drifted and then he slept, deeply and quietly, with a small smile. And Helenus and Cassandra cradled him between them and warmed him with their bodies and watched him sleep.

Getting in and out of the bell tent was a bit of a scramble and Gwin emerged on her hands and knees to find herself facing a small pair of oxblood red Dr Martens boots. She followed them up to a pair of thin legs, in what were almost certainly Primark yellow leggings. Then there was a doublet, faux Shakespearean, in shiny pleather. Above that a worried face with freckles, framed by two stiff plaits of ginger hair.

Kit and clothing were supposed to be aspirational, players adding to their costume as they progressed with the game, and the more experienced or committed ones were truly staggering, some better than re-enactors or cosplayers, and yet a sort of meld of both hobbies. New players just needed enough to get through their first event. Gwin was a new player but had been discussing the game with Beth for ages, and also had a background in historical research, worked in film, and had a bit of disposable income, so she had managed to turn up looking like someone who had been playing for a year, rather than a day. What she was looking at was a proper newbie though – the real deal.

Gwin straightened up and dusted herself down. 'Hello,' she said.

The girl was slowly swimming towards her across an ocean of social anxiety. 'Hello,' she squeaked.

'From the League?' asked Gwin.

The girl nodded furiously, screwed up her courage, held out a folded piece of paper and said, 'I'm looking for Guardian Thaddeus, this is for him.'

Gwin looked at her. 'Well, he isn't here at the moment, but I can give it to him.'

The girl looked totally flummoxed, so Gwin decided to ease the pressure. 'OC, er…out-of-character – I play him, but I'm not in character yet.'

'Oh, that's good. Er, OC-out-of-character that's good,' said the girl.

Gwin reached out and took the note from the girl's hand and opened it. Oddly, it felt like parchment, and the writing was in dipped ink, rather than biro or pencil. Someone was making an effort. Gwin read, *We have to meet, 11 o'clock, by the House of Seven Mirrors, the League. TBT.*

Icey chills made her skin crawl. The bread thieves. She looked around at the sea of tents, of the gaggles of Highguard players dressed in random bits of kit to play enemy orcs in the morning's battle. How was this even possible?

She fixed on the girl. 'Where did come from? Who gave this to you?'

'It was a…' The girl struggled to find the word, then remembered, 'A courier, from…from…' She looked at Gwin with wild desperation. 'The people who live in woods…'

'Navarr?'

'Yes! Yes, them.'

'Is that usual?'

'They walk the…er…roads…'

'The trods.'

'Yes, them, and carry messages for people, because there isn't a post office.'

'Did the courier tell you that?'

'No, I asked my friend. Er, OC-out of-character I asked my friend. Er, are we in-character or out-of-character?' The girl tailed off.

'Sort of half-in, half out,' said Gwin absently. "TBT", *how was that even possible*?

She made a concerted effort and smiled at the girl. 'Thank you.'

'That's okay.' The girl blushed. 'Sorry, I'm not supposed to say "okay". Er, OC-out-of-character sorry, I'm not supposed to say okay. Er, IC-in-character that is…er…well.'

Gwin was entirely lost for words. The girl looked at her, not sure what to do next, then realised she had done what she had to, and turned uncertainly to walk away, tripped over a guy line and fell heavily, sprawling in the grass.

'Oh my goodness!' Gwin rushed to help her up. 'Are you hurt?'

The girl was winded and had caught her shin on a tent peg. Gwin helped her to her feet and helped her hop to the bench beside the trestle table.

'Ow, ow, ow!'

Gwin sat the girl down and checked her over. There were grass stains on the knees of her leggings and the heels of her hands, but nothing seemed to be seriously damaged. 'What's your name?' She asked.

'IC-in-character or OC-out-of-character?'

'We are now out of character.' Gwin felt as though her brain might explode.

'Chaz.'

'Chaz?'

'Yes, er…Charity,' said Charity, rubbing her shin.

'Which do you prefer?'

'Everyone calls me Chaz.'

'I see. Hello Charity, I'm Gwin.'

Charity smiled shyly. 'Hi.'

'It's short for Guinevere,' said Gwin before Charity could ask.

'Wow, you should be Dawnish!'

'Not while there's breath in my body. What's your character called?'

'Violetta van Holberg.'

'Nice.'

'I think it might be a mistake, everybody keeps saying "Viennetta" and making ice cream jokes.'

'I like your doublet,' said Gwin, who didn't, but was trying to be supportive.

'Thanks, I got it on eBay,' said Charity tugging at the pleather hem.

'Yes, I thought you might have. Do you mind?' She straightened and tightened the doublet, pulling and puffing Charity's sleeves and adjusting the collarless granddad shirt she was wearing underneath. 'That shirt is good.'

'Thanks, I borrowed it from my brother.'

'Hang on to it.'

Charity coloured; the girl could blush for England. Gwin unfastened the top of the doublet and the buttons of the shirt and pulled the doublet open. Charity's hand immediately shot up and she started to pull the now plunging neckline closed. Gwin good-naturedly slapped her hand away. 'Stop that. Your character is femm…er girly?'

'Yes.'

Gwin eyed Charity's pigtails. There were yellow ribbons at the ends and the effect was definitely more Anne of Green Gables than swaggering bravo. Gwin pictured the crowded, sophisticated streets of Holberg and concluded that no Leaguer over the age of potty training would be seen dead like that – unless they were being very ironic, or extremely naughty. She removed the ribbons, unbuttoned Charity's shirt cuff, slipped the ribbons through the buttonholes, letting them hang, and folded back the sleeves two turns on either side. It was a bit like doing something for World Books Day. 'No kit shaming,' Gwin reminded herself, 'Everyone has to start somewhere.'

'Wait here,' she instructed Charity, and scrambled back into the tent, rummaged around, and emerged with her see-through ScreenFace go-bag, which she plonked on the table next to Charity. Charity studied the bag with interest.

'That's really smart.'

'Professional makeup artist.'

'Is that what you do?'

'No, but I know a few.'

'Goodness.'

'Do you wear much makeup,' asked Gwin, knowing already what the answer would be. Charity shook her head.

'Well, Violetta does,' said Gwin. 'A bit of foundation – this isn't quite your colour, but it's not far off. Just a bit, then blur it in, then a bit of powder. This is Mac and costs a fortune, but their consultations are fantastic, and the stuff is great. You can probably do just as well at Boots if you tell them what it's for.'

Gwin's big brush darted over Charity's face. 'Right, this is where we go all Leaguish – eyeliner and eyeshadow. She set up a small makeup mirror where Charity could see it. 'Watch how I'm doing this, heavy enough, but not too much – Soft Cell, not Alice Cooper. Sorry, I'm into Eighties music. Not all zombie, walking dead, okay?'

'That looks amazing!' said Charity, peering in the mirror.

'Kissing lips.'

'What?'

'Make kissing lips.'

Charity had to think about this, then obliged. Gwin dabbed on a little rouge with a fingertip. 'Now rub your lips.' She caught Charity's hand just in time. 'Rub your lips *together*.'

Charity did, and Gwin tidied up the result with a fingertip, then dabbed a touch of the rouge on each cheek and blurred it in, then stepped back to examine her work. She was not a makeup artist, but for a dabbler she was no slouch. That worked.

'Right!' She removed the elastics from Charity's braids and slipped them on to her wrist, then re-set them at the top of each braid, before rummaging in the bag for a big hairbrush and brushing out the plaits. Charity's hair had been tightly braided for three days, possibly, thought Gwin, for eighteen years, and it exploded into two auburn cascades under the brush. Gwin stood her up and examined the new Violetta.

'*Damn* girl, you've been weaponised. That hair is to die for!'

'It's not very practical,' said Charity dubiously.

'Nope, and neither is wearing twenty pounds of chainmail. Trust me, that's gonna get Violetta van Holberg seriously noticed. Is Violetta a cicisbeo?'

Charity didn't recognise the term at first and had to think about it. When the penny finally dropped, Gwin, who was being mischievous, thought the girl might actually spontaneously combust or at least burst a blood vessel.

'*NO!* I mean, *no*, no she isn't. She's a…a…'

'Bravo?'

'Yes, one of those.'

'Have you got a sword?'

Charity shook her head. 'They said it was best to buy one here, and I looked, but they are quite expensive.'

'Are you coming back? Coming to the next event?'

Charity nodded wildly. 'Absolutely, this weekend has been amazing, I mean probably the best one ever in my whole life!'

'Okay.' Gwin disappeared into the tent again and emerged with Thaddeus's shortsword and belt. 'I bought this online, but I was lucky, it passed weapon inspection – you can see it's got a coloured rubber band on it. I'm going to replace it though. You have it.' Gwin buckled the belt around Charity's waist and adjusted the sword.

'I couldn't!' said Charity, stunned.

'It's good luck to keep kit circulating. When you've finished with it, you pass it on too.'

Charity drew the sword and waved it around inexpertly.

'Promise me you'll go on Vinted or something, as soon as you get back, and find a pair of pre-loved over the knee boots?'

Charity shook her head. 'No, I would never wear them.'

'No, you wouldn't, but Violetta will, in fact she'll never take them off, even in bed.' Gwin considered for a moment. 'Especially in bed.' She fixed Charity with a hard stare.

'Er, okay,' said Charity with a giggle.

'Give me your phone,' said Gwin. She took the phone and photographed the new, improved Violetta, then passed the phone to Charity, who stared at the picture open-mouthed.

She gave Gwin a hug. 'How do you know makeup artists?'

'I work in the film industry.'

'*Seriously*?'

'Yes.'

'Have you ever met anyone famous?'

'Not really, I'm mostly in admin. Do you work?'

'Yes, in a pet superstore.'

'Bunnies?'

'Reptiles mostly. I have a lizard.'

'Really? You do have a dark side.'

'His name's Rex.'

'As in T-rex?'

'How do you know that?'

'Wild guess. You had better get back to the League, they'll be sending out a search party,' said Gwin, who knew they wouldn't. 'And don't forget, swagger!'

Charity gave her another hug. 'Can I friend you?'

'If you must. Now swagger along.'

And Charity swaggered away, stopping to turn and wave every few paces.

'For heaven's sake, look out for ropes and tent pegs!' Gwin shouted at her as she waved her on her way.

Gwin-as-Thaddeus wandered through the tents towards the League. In the adjacent field, the battle was generating a roar of voices like the sound of an ocean. She stopped a player in League costume and asked which was the House of Seven Mirrors tent and was pointed towards a big double bell tent at the end of a row. She strode towards the tent and suddenly found her way blocked by four players, Navarr from their woodland costume, worryingly, their faces were covered. The nearest stepped towards her and she reached for her shortsword, realising with a sick feeling of horror that she no longer had it. He was wearing a green and black shemagh over his head and most of his face, and only his eyes and wire-rimmed glasses were visible.

'Venom blade,' he said and held out his hand threateningly.

Gwin looked. He was holding a larp-safe throwing knife, pointed towards her like a dagger. Being larp safe, the blade was thicker than a real dagger and soft. Being designed as a throwing knife it lacked the fibreglass and Kevlar core of other larp weapons, as a result the chubby little thing drooped in a way that was positively indecent.

Gwin looked down at the knife, up at the would-be assassin, and back down to the knife, then seized his wrist, twisted his hand so quickly he shouted with surprise, and drove the soft rubber blade into his chest. He looked down with astonishment, then obligingly fell to his knees and started role-playing death-by-venomed-blade. As he did so Gwin caught a movement in her peripheral vision and swerved at the waist like a matador as a big elaborate dagger swished past. She reached, snatched it out her second assailant's hand and slashed it across his throat. He was just as astonished as her first attacker but played the game and fell forward fingers clawing at his throat. Gwin had picked up a few useful moves.

Thaddeus hefted the dagger in his hand, turned around and felt a heavy blow to his stomach that knocked the breath out of him. The dagger fell from his fingers. Nimble, and quick as lightening, the other assassins had circled behind him while he was fighting the first two. Thaddeus looked down, expecting to see a clenched fist in his midriff. But the blow wasn't a punch, he had been stabbed, a jewelled hilt in a gloved hand. The attacker slowly drew out the long blade, smeared with Thaddeus's blood and some blue oily liquid. Then plunged the dagger into Thaddeus again and this time he knew what it was and felt the pain and cried out. His legs were numb, and he fell to his knees. The assassin stooped and drove the knife home one last time, upwards, at the base of Thaddeus's breastbone, the killing blow.

Paralysis was claiming Thaddeus as he slumped on his knees in front of his killer. His heart was racing, desperately trying to pump his dwindling blood around his body, and with every beat spreading the venom through his veins. He stared up at his killer and tried to form a word. 'Who?'

Who had killed him? Was it one of the twins' other lovers, driven by jealousy? Was it his chapter enemies from the chapel taking the law into their own hands? The phrase 'there will be a reckoning' swam into his mind. *Rodrigo*?

Thaddeus couldn't close his eyes, but his sight began to darken. The killer put his hand to Thaddeus's shoulder and pushed him over, to lie on his back in the spreading pool of blood. As he died, Thaddeus realised he wasn't joining a queue of virtuous souls heading for the Labyrinth and eventual rebirth. For that matter, there were no gardens or drinking halls filled with fallen heroes. For him, there was only black oblivion, and as it embraced him, he was grateful.

The last sound he heard were his assassins telling him, 'He said…He said you would understand.'

'You do understand, don't you?' The words caught on a sob. Thaddeus heard the voices and, for one final time, surrendered to them.

XVI

Beth was fuming. 'Seriously, as soon as we get back, I'm going to email and complain. I mean a proper formal complaint – you can't just murder someone's character at their first event. I'm going to see if I can get him reinstated.'

'You and Russell said people lose their characters in the first skirmish of the event. At least that didn't happen.'

'Yes, but that's almost like an accident. I mean your character was *murdered*.'

'Thaddeus was into some really serious stuff, and he knew it.'

'Gwin, no he wasn't, he did one skirmish, one battle and went shopping!'

'Which way?'

'The drive though,' said Beth, pointing, as they turned off the roundabout.

'In the glove box, there's some vouchers,' said Gwin. Beth rummaged in the clutter and found a strip of vouchers.

Gwin leant out of the window to make herself heard. 'Six chicken nuggets, medium fries and a large strawberry shake.' She turned to Beth who nodded. 'And a double cheeseburger meal, medium, with a coke.'

They moved forward to the window to pay and Gwin realised she didn't have her phone or cards in reach. 'Don't worry,' said Beth, 'I'll get this,' and leant across her.

'Don't forget these!' said Gwin and tore off two vouchers.

They collected the food and drinks from the next window, Gwin piled them on Beth and drove around the car park until she found a space. They fell on their food in companionable silence.

'The thing is,' said Beth screwing up the wrapper of her cheeseburger, 'There's so much for you to learn about Empire, I mean you barely scratched the surface. I wish you had really *experienced* it!'

Gwin smiled to herself. 'You okay if we get going? I don't want to catch the traffic.' She handed Beth her rubbish. 'Could you dump this in the bin?'

They pulled out of the car park and Gwin suddenly remembered her phone and cards. 'Can you reach the big Tesco bag behind my seat, the yellow one?' she asked. 'I think my cards and phone are still in the pouch on my belt.'

'Belt?'

'Yes, the skinny black belt with the pouch on it. I gave my sword belt to someone.'

'Got it! Two pouches,' Beth corrected her as she struggled to reach the belt and pull it out of the bag.

'*Two* pouches?' queried Gwin.

'Yes, the big one shaped like a shell and the little coin purse one.'

Gwin felt the chills again. She stared out through the windscreen. There were raindrops, she flicked on the wipers.

'Beth – the little pouch, what's in it?'

Beth slumped back down in her seat, arranged the belt on her lap and struggled to untie the drawcord of the pouch. 'Nothing.'

Gwin was disappointed. 'Nothing?'

'Just a few crumbs, bits of old bread.'

Gwin grinned. 'He's done it again. He always does that!'

'What are you talking about?'

'A sort of message.'

'You've totally lost me. Gwin, do you think you'll come back again. I know this weekend's been a bit of a bust. I'm so sorry, especially as you got all your kit and everything.'

'Beth,' said Gwin, 'This weekend has been totally magical, and I will *definitely* come again.'

'You'll need a new character though.'

'Yes, I will, won't I?'

XVII

Gwin woke up, and, for once, knew exactly where she was. She also knew that the arm holding her, and the body pressed against hers were Zac's. She could tell by his breathing, he was asleep. She shifted slightly, and Zac's arm tightened, pulling her against him, her back pressed against his chest. Gwin considered the situation, and decided she liked it very much. She gave a little wriggle, and that sleeping reflex hugged her still tighter, and his knees pressed against the back of hers. *Just like spoons*, she thought. There was, though, an issue. She was hungry, and to prove the point, her stomach gave a growl. Calories had been burnt. Epic amounts of calories had been burnt. Gwin realised that if she stayed in bed, Zac would wake up, and rally, and then there would be delays. This was the moment for moral fibre, for decisive action. Leadership was required.

She gently lifted his arm and slipped out from underneath, and out of bed. She found his T-shirt from yesterday on the floor. It was too big by exactly the right amount, and smelt of him, which was nice. She walked around to his side of the bed. He had shifted, his face was in the dip in the pillow where her head had been, his arm stretched out for her. She kissed his shoulder, he didn't move. Gwin knew she had ruined him, broken him, the poor lamb. She sang a little song to herself. It wasn't very tuneful or complicated, and it mostly went "la-la-la", but it caught her mood perfectly.

Gwin went downstairs, and with her newly acquired confidence, started going through Zac's kitchen cupboards and examining the contents of his fridge. Joy-of-joys, there was bacon. Everything was there, tidy, clean, and not very much used by the look of it. She found a frying pan, and soon the little house was full of the smell of frying bacon. She clattered around finding plates and mugs.

Suddenly, Zac was standing in the kitchen doorway. He had a towelling robe on, his hair was standing up, and he had a shadow of stubble. He wasn't lounging, or leaning against the doorway, but standing framed, like a small boy on Christmas morning confronted by a pile of wondrous gifts under the tree. He couldn't take his eyes of her. 'What are you doing?' he finally asked.

'Bacon sandwiches.'

'Gwin, I, I mean, that is, I think I'm…'

She shushed him with a finger to his lips. 'Red sauce or brown.'

'Brown. Gwin I…'

'Tea or coffee?' She was brandishing two canisters she'd found.

'Coffee. Not that one – this…' Zac indicated a machine in the corner.

'You'll have to do it then; I don't know how it works.'

Zac busied himself with the machine, which clicked and whirred and gurgled out a mug full. 'Do you want one?'

'Yes please, the same as yours.' The bacon crackled and sizzled.

The toaster popped up two more slices and Gwin juggled them onto a plate and started assembling sandwiches, being lavish with the sauces. She handed the stunned Zac a plate with a sandwich and his mug of coffee. 'I thought we could eat them in bed.' Zac turned and obediently retraced his footsteps up the stairs. Gwin helped herself to a few pieces of kitchen towel, grabbed her coffee and sandwich and followed him up. As she climbed the stairs, she sent a telepathic message to Cassandra and Helenus, wherever they were, thanking the gorgeous, clever, murderous little poppets, and promising that if their paths ever crossed in the future, she was buying the drinks.

Gwin and Zac sat up in bed, and she demolished her bacon sandwich, the plate under her chin to catch all the ketchup. 'I always say it helps to start the day...with breakfast.'

Zac had taken one bite from his sandwich, and just kept looking at her.

He seemed to be assembling some great truth, struggling to find the words to articulate it. He finally spoke, 'I didn't know...I had no idea. I never, ever, *imagined* it could be so good.' He was staring at her as if she might dematerialise in a shower of sparkles. Gwin wasn't looking at him, but straight down the bed, where her feet were sticking out from the duvet. She wiggled all her toes and allowed herself a big grin – but mostly on the side of her face he couldn't see.

'The important thing,' she said with studied innocence, 'is not overcooking the bacon.'